Intro

How did I meet this fool? I can barely remember.
I had to really think about it for a hot minute. Hmmmm.
Oh yes, after the club one night while parking lot
pimping…

My girlfriend and I were leaning hard against the
hood of the car, checking out the scenery. This guy
approaches and my girl seems to know him, somewhat.
She was friendly, but I could definitely tell it was not *that*
kind of friendliness. When I heard his voice I realized he
was the same dude I heard earlier walking behind us and
talking to his boy as we left the club and headed to our
car. He was polite and funny. He didn't turn me on, but
he didn't turn me off, either. So I scoped out the
landscape. Nice build, medium sized dude. Fair skinned,
fresh hair cut like I like. Outfit was on point and his shoes
were right. Ok, I might be able to do this. Let's see how
this goes. Within a minute or two he turns to me and says
"What's up?" I smile and reply nicely, "Nothing. What
you up to tonight?"

"We tryna go eat. Y'all wanna come?" Of course I'm
down for a candlelit breakfast at the Waffle House so I
turn to my girl who gives me the unspoken – hell yeah!

"Yeah, let's go. We'll follow y'all."

We head to the Waffle House and all sit down and
get ready to order. He brought a couple friends and it's
me and a couple of my girlfriends. I got the low down on
the ride over. *He's a dope boy and he likes to flaunt - so*

order whatever you want because he is going to pay for everyone's food. That's just how he does it. I'm thinking, ok, cool. I start with OJ and waffles; bacon and eggs and one biscuit on the side with strawberry jam. From me, the waitress makes her way around the table and within a couple minutes she has everyone's order and is off to the back.

Ole boy is true to his reputation. He orders steak and eggs and flaunts his money as he pays for everyone's meal. Man, had I known then what I know now I would have run for the freakin' hills. For more reasons than one. Dudes that flaunt like that are never good news and they're usually not doing it nearly as big as they'd like you to think. But I was young and dumb and soon I'd be full of cum too and strung out over this abusive fool. By the end of the night I was leaving the Waffle House in his car and waving bye to my friends. Little did I know the real ride I was about to take.

So we get to his place and I find out it's not actually *his* place, but his boy's place. Again, young and dumb. I would start to count the red flags, but I'd surely loose count and the number is massive. So I'll skip it. We get inside and its a'ight. Nothing spectacular. Nothing too bad either. Just a regular townhouse. I did have enough good sense about me to tell him in the car that there would be no booty given or received that night. "I just met you and I don't know your ass from Adam. You could be a serial killer." That led to us laughing and talking and watching TV all night. I finally fell asleep and when I woke up the next morning I smelled bacon from downstairs.

As I approached the stairwell I heard voices so I stopped dead in my tracks. I heard his voice, but there was also another male voice, and a girl's voice laughing in the background. I went back upstairs and waited patiently. I didn't know what this dude was like outside the parking lot of a nightclub and the Waffle House, but I knew I wasn't trying to meet his friends like that. I knew they would've thought he got the tail. I'm not tryna do the walk of shame when I didn't even get any last night. After a while I heard the door open and then close and I heard a car leave. The voices subsided and he came upstairs and told me to come down and have some breakfast. I did as I was told and enjoyed the food and the fresh sunlight.

As I ate I began my interrogation. I have always been curious. Some may say downright nosey, but I needs ta know. Ya know? Who is this dude? What is he about? Why is he trying to get up on me? What's up with his dope boy status and his flaunting when he's hanging out at his boy's place with me? Is he married, on the run, got a girlfriend back at his place? What? And on top of all that I knew I would be screwing him soon enough so I wanted to know BEFORE we headed down that path. I ate. I asked. He answered. He lied his ass off. He was helping his boy out which is why we came there last night. He lived alone on the other side of town. He didn't have any kids. He was single. He worked. Wait a damn minute! "You work?" "Where?" "What do you do for a living?" "Do you sell drugs?" Yeah, that's how stupid I was. I asked the man did he sell drugs for a living? Who does that? My young naive ass, that's who.

Needless to say, breakfast was over at that point and he told me he'd take me home. I gathered my things and went outside to his car. When he put the car in reverse he asked me where I lived. I told him and he took off in that direction. We're driving and he's telling me how pretty I am and how fine I am. I'm smiling and soaking it all up. Then he asked me why I wouldn't let him hit it? Who does that? His inappropriate ass, that's who. I went through my serial killer speech again, but he wasn't buying it. He kept asking until I finally told him. "Why would I do you on the first night? So you can drop me off today and not call me again and I can feel like a lil' hoe! I'm not screwing you on the first night. Period. You or any other dude. You can just drop me off at my house." The rest of the ride was in silence. I didn't know what it meant and really I didn't care. It wasn't that serious to me. I got a meal last night, breakfast this morning, a ride home and I hadn't given up anything. He wasn't all that cute any damn way! How are you gonna pressure me *after* the fact? That's crazy as hell.

We got to my house and he pulled up nice and slow. "You gonna give me your number?" I looked at him completely puzzled. This negro wants my number after that? Whatever!

"Yeah, it's 555-5555."

"A'ight, Imma call you."

"OK"

And that was my introduction to Messy Marvin. This would become one of the most twisted interactions I would ever experience with a member of the opposite sex. He would later become permanently imbedded in my psyche as a complete and utter monster and a very, very disturbed individual. He would evolve into a vicious abuser who tried his damndest to trample my self worth and dishonor me in every imaginable way. That was how I met this crazed man who would eventually try to kill me.

Chapter 1

Fast forward about a month and you'd find me in that same apartment we went to the first night we met. His *boy's* place. I was already sick of the place. I didn't understand why the hell we couldn't go to his place and I was starting to get tired of the paneling on the walls and the nasty brown, left over 70's looking shag carpeting. I hated being there. We were confined to the one bedroom upstairs because being anywhere else in the place felt like an intrusion. Not only was it his boy's place, but his boy's girlfriend lived there too. So you have 4 people, 2 couples piled up in a small 2 bedroom apartment. Oh and have I told you that I had yet to meet his boy. Yeah, we were hold up in that damn room on some Anne Frank type shit. I was over it. "Why we always gotta be up in here? Let's go to your house. I don't get it. What's the problem?"

"The problem is you ain't gave me dat ass yet. You can't go to my house until we fuck."

"You think that shit is funny? You ain't funny. What does that have to do with your house anyway?"

"I'm just playing, but you do need to get up off that ass. For real. I ain't gonna keep waitin' and shit."

"So that's how you ask? You can't do better than that?"

"Come here then. Let me kiss you."

And like that we went from not fucking to fucking. See this is where things started to get sticky. For me anyway. But what happened was some straight Ike Turner type business. He pulled me across the bed by the small of my back. He made sure I was very close to him. He put his lips on my lips and we began kissing. You know that moment when a kiss goes from a kiss to damn, this is some realness? Yeah, right then, at that moment he stopped. He pulled his face back from mine and said, "Well I guess Imma have to teach you how to kiss. You don't know what you doing." Who the hell does that, like that? Thinking back now I remember feeling something drop inside myself. The feeling went from somewhere between my throat and my heart right down to the pit of my belly. It landed with a thud and I was lost. I felt confused. I had never experienced that feeling before and I couldn't identify it. It wasn't in my realm of knowledge before that moment. He had just introduced me to what I call the taking of my spirit. That was the first blow and they would keep coming like that. Blow by blow, like tiny little grenades that would explode all around my heart and soul and eat away at the edges of my soul.

He felt my hesitation and as soon as he felt me begin to pull away, he forced my body forward towards his again so that I couldn't move or process what was going on in my mind or my body. He put his lips on mine again and said, "do like I do. You don't know how to do this right so I have to show you." All this in the midst of this whirlwind going on in my head. I didn't know what to do or how to do so I followed the instructions I was given.

2

That's how it begins. Those miniscule moments like that are the first tiny rips of you from your awareness. From your consciousness. People often ask, how could that be? How could a woman do this or that or stay here or there? They don't realize that you are not you. You are so far removed and disassembled that you are no longer yourself. You are these fragmented pieces all over the place because you're not allowed those brief moments to process these unfamiliar feelings and remain whole. So the unfamiliar, defragmented version becomes the body in which you now move throughout the world. That shit is crazy.

After he finished kissing me he made me lie down on the bed. He took off all my clothes and we had sex. Just like that. It was not a bad thing. It was not vicious or painful or any of those things. It was just ... sex. It was not erotic or intimate or romantic. It was robotic and it was simply ok. It was very similar to how I felt when I first laid eyes on him. I wasn't totally turned on, but I wasn't totally turned off either. It was *meh*.

When the act was finished he went into the bathroom and turned on the shower. In a minute or so I could hear him step into the water. I think he was washing himself. When he finished he called for me, "come get in here with me." Now I had showered with a guy before. I wasn't completely inexperienced, but I wasn't feeling him like that. Our interactions had never really been romantic or particularly intimate and to me, something like showering with a man was an act that had been romanticized in my world. That was all prior to Messy Marvin, though.

3

"I don't want to." I called back.

"Why? What's wrong with you?"

"Nothing. I'm just really shy about my body. I don't want to." I wasn't really shy about my body. I just didn't want to be in the shower with him.

"Girl, c'mon. We just fucked! I already saw your body. I'm not gonna do anything to you. I will look away while you get in. Since you scared." He was taunting me.

Reluctantly I got up and started to move toward the bathroom. I mean, he did have a point. He *had* already seen my body. What was the big deal? When I got to the shower he was indeed turned around so that he was not facing me. But as soon as I got in he turned to face me. I slapped his shoulder. "You said you wouldn't look!"

"Girl stop playing! I wanna see you." He took a step back and looked me up and down. Turned me around and looked at me from behind, then from the front. He pushed me back gently so that I was about arm's distance away from him. He took one step back away from me and just starred at me. "Put your arms down so I can see you! You're so childish! What you scared of?"

"I don't know. I told you I was shy! Why do you keep asking me that?"

"Hmph, you ain't as fine as I first thought you were. Your ass isn't as round and nice as I thought. Your titties ain't all that either. You a'ight, but I thought you looked way better than this. I been waiting all this time and thinking you were super fine and you just a'ight."

I wanted to run the hell out of that shower, bathroom, apartment, his life! I was so embarrassed. So ashamed. I didn't have any issues with the way I looked. I never really had. I was petite with nice brown skin. I had always had full lips and a track runner's body. I had a six pack, muscular calves and thighs and a nice round booty. He was just being plain ole mean.

"Fuck you! I look good and your ass wasn't complaining a few minutes ago when you were bouncing up and down on it! Get out the damn shower so I can bathe."

This was the first time I can remember making a mental excuse for his inappropriate behavior. He got out of the shower and I thought to myself, he's just trying to make a joke. He thinks he's funny that's why he said that. He's just being stupid. But in my belly was that same feeling again and it hit with a thud for the second time in one day.

So I'd swept all these initial signs under the rug and am now in a relationship with this person. Fast forward again a few more months and the truth about his "living situation" comes to light. The truth of the matter was that he did not have a place to live. He was bouncing back and forth between his mother's house and his *boy's* place. This is where I started to really get in deep. At some point I knew that Marvin didn't have his own place and that when I saw him I would have to spend time at his friend's place. So I'm into this relationship when he comes to me and tells me that he wants us to move in together. I am shocked because I am still living with my mom and this grown ass man is living with… whomever - at the moment. His explanation was that he wanted to be with me 24-7. When that doesn't fly with me he takes it to the next level – "If you care about me and I need help with something, why don't you want to help me?" Huh? What the hell? 'Need' me? How so? I don't understand. After he blows up because I keep resisting I finally, finally learn the truth. This negro has no credit, poor rental history and not enough money to get him past those first 2 hurdles and 'needs' my young dumb ass in order to get an apartment. Pitiful, I know. At the time I thought it didn't really matter. I wanted to live with him anyway. By this time, we had developed a kind of routine and I had gotten used to him and he was accustomed to me too. I figured it wouldn't be a big deal so that lame excuse worked and I agreed to get *us* an apartment in my name. The agreement was that he would pay the bills and I would go to school full time. So I should be set up pretty well, right? Dating a dope boy with a box Chevy, he's paying the bills on what is technically MY apartment and I'm getting school behind me all at the same damn time. Not so fast.

So first off, this fool had to be THEE worst drug dealer in history. We never had the liquid cash flow you'd think would be present, we shared ONE car, the apartment was one notch above the apartment complex from the cartoon the PJ's and I ended up having to work AND go to school because "ya boy" needed 'help.' This some bullshit here and just wrong on so many levels. In addition to all of the above, moving in together is when the viciousness and abuse escalated. It started out slowly and eventually took off to the moon! There were little things that seemed to bother him that were just so foreign to me. If I said "good morning" when we woke in the morning he would intentionally not respond. The first few times I blew it off by telling myself that maybe he just wasn't a morning person. Making more excuses for him in my head. One morning he exploded. I offered my usual "good morning" punctuated with a smile. He went off, "Why the fuck do you always have to say that stupid shit! What's so damn *good* about it anyway? Don't nobody want to hear that shit and don't nobody wake up saying that stupid shit! You always bouncing around here all early in the fucking morning! Sit the fuck down some God Damn where!" As I had now become accustomed to doing, I refrained from doing what came naturally to me. I mean, who doesn't say good morning to the person they share a home with? That's crazy to me. So I just stopped saying anything in the mornings. It wasn't worth the energy it took to listen to him rant. This wouldn't be the last time I'd smother something that felt natural to me. There'd be many more times I'd have to suffocate my natural impulses to keep the peace and the teeth in my mouth.

About 6-8 months into this living arrangement, Messy Marvin had taken to a 9-5 job to help pay the bills. His 9-5 was placing and removing orange cones from construction areas. This shit is really sad, but unfortunately it gets worse. Despite all his craziness and emotional instability, he did have some characteristics that were redeeming. He was very strict with himself about how he maintained his living space and his body. I don't know if this was left over from prison or the military, because he'd done time in both places, but it seemed to give him some comfort. Every night he packed his lunch and put it in the refrigerator. He ironed his clothes and laid them out every single night. He even ironed his underwear and laid them out as well. His keys were placed next to the stand at the front door and he ate the same pistachio ice cream Every. Single. Night. after dinner. He was also NEVER, EVER late to work. Looking back I think it's weird as all get out (especially the underwear thing) in comparison to the person I thought I'd met a year or so earlier, but it was something else I had gotten used to. One night when he was making his lunch he called for me to come into the kitchen. I went in and he was standing there holding the multi-pack of mini bags of chips. He was just standing there starring at the bag. When I asked what was wrong, he said "Where are the Doritos?" I have no idea and honestly I think this whole scene is kind of funny. I replied, "I don't know. Why don't you just take a different one tomorrow?"

"Cause I want the fucking Doritos!" Oh Lord, here we go again with this craziness. Why can't he just let it go? I'm so not in the mood for this crap tonight.

"I really don't know. I don't eat them and I haven't touched the pack since you bought it." I'm walking away as I say this because at this point I'm thinking this is some real live bullshit that I don't feel like dealing with at the moment.

"Bring your ass back here right now! I want my God damn Doritos! I want my fucking Doritos!"

This fool is screaming at the top of his lungs. He sounds like he's outside on the playground and I feel like a kindergarten teacher who has a student throwing a temper tantrum. I slowly walk back to the kitchen because I have learned that irritating him with non-compliance only makes things worse. When I make my way back to the screaming I lean up against the door jam of the kitchen door and cross one leg over the other. He's in a full on rage. Screaming, pacing back and forth, flinging the pack of chips across the room, just straight up madness over some damn chips. At this time I was not afraid of him in the way that I would soon become. I pretty much knew how to deal with his outbursts and I did so when I had to and once it was over, I went back to what had become my new normal. In the midst of this he manages to look over and see me leisurely leaning against the door looking at him. Apparently this pissed him off because he dropped the pack of chips, came up to me and slapped me down to the ground. Literally. He hit me so hard I was stunned for a moment. I was out of my head, dazed and I had no idea how that had happened the way it had. I was on the floor on all fours and I had to shake my head back and forth to get my wits about me. When I looked up he was standing over me looking down on me like Ali did Sonny Liston. I was still a little dazed and things were a little bit blurry, but I knew I'd better get up quickly or being beaten while down would be my fate, for sure. I had learned that lesson the first time he'd hit me. He still had that enraged look on his face when I looked up from the floor the second time.

Months earlier I had gone to the club with my girl. I was over this Marvin situation. He was working midnights picking up cones. (That's just funny no matter how you look at it) My girl found out that there was something going on and the DJ was one who was sure to deliver. So I get dressed, get my hair did, avoid this fool's phone calls and make my way to the club. The added bonus was that this dude I had been trying to push up on for a minute would likely be in the club. Let's do this!! I'm in the club with my girl, we have our pitcher of sex-on-the-beach, the music is dead on, the place is packed AND dude is in here tonight. Hell to da yeah! A good time was had by all. After we get it together, we find a ride home from the club. I was living with my mom at the time. She was out of town and I had the house to myself. I walk up to the front door and as soon as I stepped into the house I had a really weird feeling come over me. Never ever ignore that feeling. Never. I would offer that advice to anyone. The house was super quiet and it just felt eerie. I walked in slowly and looked around the living room. Nothing. Next I checked the kitchen and pantry area. Again, nothing. Then I went back outside and looked around the driveway that led up to the front door. Nothing. *What the hell is going on* - is all I was thinking. This shit is weird as hell. I went back into the house and slowly walked down the hall.

There were four bedrooms that broke off from the hallway. I was too spooked to go into each room so I just walked slowly and closed each door as I passed it. You know how the person in the movies who goes into the room looking always ends up impaled to the wall by a wooden stake? Not tryna have that happen to me. I reached the last two bedrooms. One to the right and the other to the left. The room to the left was the master bedroom - my mother's bedroom. There was an attached bathroom in that bedroom. The bathroom had a small window and that was a scary thought because that window opened up to the back yard which was pitch black at this time of night. Damn I'm scared to go in there.

The bedroom on the right was my bedroom and there were 2 windows in that room. One window was low to the ground and almost spanned the length of the wall. If someone wanted to, they really could 'get me' in this house. Damn! As I approached the end of the hall I noticed my foot locker from college sitting there in the middle of the floor. Completely out of place. That foot locker was never there. Right then I remembered that I had pulled it out of my room the day before and left it at the end of the hallway. I'm going crazy in here. Am I still drunk? This is some Freddy Krueger type shit. I'm really scared as hell. Just when I had almost talked myself into believing that I was just freaking out for no reason I noticed something. For real this time. There atop my foot locker sat a set of keys. Whose keys are these and why are they in my house? What the hell is going on here? So like the girl in the movie who is about to be killed next, I start screaming at whoever the heck it is that is in my house tryna kill me. "I know you are in here! You might as well come out now because I know something is going on!" Has this shit ever worked? Hell no! But I was scared and your mind goes to another place. Of course I didn't get a response so I ran to the kitchen to use the phone that was in there. I called my girl who had made it home by now. I was asking her if she remembered seeing anything funny when they dropped me off, but she didn't have a clue either.

Ok, this was getting me nowhere. I hung up and forced myself to walk back down the hall. By this time I had turned on every light in the house and I was treading very lightly. I looked in each bedroom and in the main bathroom. I snatched back the shower curtain in one fell swoop of my arm. Damn, nothing. I knew that meant the killer was either in my room or in my mother's room or her bathroom. I had convinced myself it was a killer and that he was after me. My room was actually easy, especially after I checked the closet. Then the horror hit me. That meant the killer was definitely in my mother's bedroom or her bathroom. Holy Shit! I walked in there and turned to the right. I had to look in the closet and pray that Mr. Murderer wasn't under the bed. There was no way in hell I was looking under the bed. If he's under there then let him get me. Damn that. Right then I heard a noise in the bathroom. A slight noise. The kind that makes you wonder whether or not you even really heard anything. I slowly made my way around the edge of the bed and started to move toward the bathroom. I heard rustling and I knew my mind was NOT playing tricks on me. "Who is in here?" I'm screaming at the dark in the doorway to the bathroom. I heard a voice and I could tell it was a male. Now let me explain how tiny this bathroom is, or rather, half bathroom. It is the size of a coat closet. There was just enough room for a toilet a sink and a window. Literally, that's all there was in the bathroom. I couldn't imagine why I wasn't already dead. I mean, all the killer had to do was jump out and he'd have me. He must be standing right there in the middle of the bathroom with his knife ready to slit my throat.

I was shaking in my boots, but I poked my head around the corner and quickly turned on the light. All I saw were feet and calves. I was starting to understand what was going on. This FOOL was hiding inside my mother's home, in her master bedroom, in the HALF bathroom, and he had lodged himself between the sink and toilet! And to top it all off, he was stuck. This is a complete FOOL if I've ever seen one. Now not only am I glad to still be alive, but I have to help this idiot get up from between the sink and the toilet. I reach over and give him my hand, which he promptly takes a hold of, and I help him up.

Once he's up all I can do is laugh. I mean, really, where they do that? I run out of the bathroom and into the bedroom and from there I take the hallway back to the living room. I am dying laughing all the damn way. You look like a fool! I'm laughing at him and I'm laughing at myself. I thought I was about to be murdered and this dumb ass is stuck in my mama's bathroom! Who does that? Straight foolishness.

I'm now in the living room sitting on the sofa and I am still cracking up. He is in front of me and he's pacing back and forth, back and forth, right in front of me. I'm sitting on the edge of the sofa and I have my face in my hands with my elbows on my knees and I'm still giggling. He says, "So you think that shit is funny, huh? Where have you been?"

"Negro how the hell did you get into this house? And where did you park your car? And why in the world were you wedged between the sink and toilet like that?" With just the thought the visual pops into my head and I start to laugh again.

"I'm a mutha fuckin' Navy seal! That's how I got in here! That shit was easy."

"A Navy Seal? Bwahahahaha! Your ass was stuck like Chuck. Kicking your feet like a baby. If I hadn't helped you up, you'd still be back there squirming. Navy Seal.....bwahahahaha!"

"Shut up or I'll knock you out! You don't think I will, do you? I will fuck you up!"

Right then I saw him draw back and he hit me with all his might. WHAP! Right across my face. He hit me so hard he knocked me from the sofa onto the floor. I hit the floor with a thump. I landed on all fours. As I was down there I saw him rip the nearby phone cord from the wall. He was in a rage, but I knew he was still thinking. I've heard women say that their abusers 'lose it' or become 'monsters' or something of that sort. Messy knew what he was doing. He was enraged, but calculated all at the same time. I didn't look up, but I knew he was watching me. I could feel the heat of his eyes on my back. He was a predator and I was his prey in that moment. He was sizing me up. Waiting to see what my next move would be. He was evaluating me as I lay there on the floor.

My reaction in that moment would set a standard and somewhere in me I had figured that out. I had heard once that if you don't fight back it gets worse. Beside all those thoughts, my natural instinct was to fight back. Fuck him up. You can't just hit me! Are you crazy? I didn't flinch or give any indication that I was going to charge his ass. Wanted to catch him off guard. I actually let my weight go and I fell forward on the floor as if to give up. He fell for it hook, line and sinker. He walked over and positioned himself in front of me. I could see his feet in front of my face. As soon as I could tell that he relaxed, I pounced. I jumped up and grabbed him around the waist and pushed against the floor with my feet as hard as I could. I charged straight into him and when he hit the wall I let go of his waist and punched him in the face as hard as I could. I could tell it stunned him in more ways than one.

So what do you do in this moment young lady? While he's there against the wall stunned: You gut punch that ass. I hit him again. He shook his head and grabbed me around my neck and flung me back onto the sofa and ran straight at me. When he got close enough I kicked him with both feet with full force. He was a thin guy so the kick put enough space between us for me to get up. I ran toward the kitchen and he read my mind. He quickly caught up to me and pushed me as he ran past me. He got to the phone in the kitchen and wrapped the cord around his hand and tore it from the wall. When I caught up to him he grabbed my face with his hand and pushed me into the sink. He held my head against the counter top with his hand still covering my face. He was yelling at me, but mentally I was spent and I couldn't even hear what he was saying. I was in survival mode. I was trying to kick, but his body was pressed close to mine and I couldn't lift my legs enough to get a good kick in. I was struggling and wiggling like crazy and one of his fingers slipped into my mouth. I bit down hard and he let go and screamed out in pain.

I was completely surprised when he ran. He just stopped and ran out of the back door of the kitchen. I was gasping for air, trying to think, my face was hurting and I had no clue where he went, why he ran so suddenly or what this meant for my safety. Was he going to get a gun? Was he coming back? Is he gone for good? Should I move or wait? Instinct kicked in. I ran to the back door he had gone out of and locked it. I ran to the front door and made sure it was locked. I ran to the side door off the living room and made sure it was locked. While in the living room I saw lights outside and heard an engine revving. I stopped cold. I just stood there. I didn't know what was going on. I just listened. I recognized the sound of the car. It was his car! Was this lunatic going to drive through my mother's living room?

He revved the engine one final time and I saw the headlights of his car pass by the window of the living room. Now it made sense. He had parked his car in my mom's backyard and broken in while I was at the club with my pitcher of sex-on-the-beach. That's why I hadn't known earlier that he was in the house. This is some crazy shit. I ran to the phone in the living room, but the cord was ripped in half. I ran to the kitchen and fumbled for a few seconds before I was able to plug the cord back into the wall and dial 911.

Chapter 2

During the time I'd spent with him I had learned a few lessons. Women of abusers learn some of these same lessons.

1. Once you're in the storm – don't fight against the wind. Just go with it.

2. The more submissive you are, the sooner it will likely be over.

3. If there is ANY way to prevent setting him off – do what it takes to prevent setting him off. AT ALL COSTS!

I didn't want to agitate him any further since the Doritos had done a sufficient job already so I just got up and went into the bathroom. I turned on the light and looked in the mirror. I had a busted lip. A little blood, but nothing too bad. I began to wash my face and draw a bath. I was still not in the mood to deal with this tonight. I was tired.

Most times if it didn't escalate, I could walk away and he would simmer in another room and let me be. This was something I'd come to know since we lived together. As long as I was in the house with him, I could diffuse the situation a lot of the time. I later learned that this was part of his psyche. He was so insecure that the only tool he had to soothe himself was control. Me living in the house with him gave him control over my physical being. He knew where I was and what I was doing 95% of the time. There was some disturbing comfort in that for him. As long as I did not resist him or fight back and as long as I stayed in the house he would not baulk if I left a heated interaction and went into another part of the apartment.

I took a long bath. A very long bath. When I decided to go ahead and get out it was because the water was cold and obviously I couldn't sit in there all night. I dried my body slowly. One arm, then the other. One leg, then the other. Like a robot on autopilot. My mind was so gone. What the hell was wrong with him that made him this way? I just didn't understand. I'd never experienced anything like this before. I let out a long sigh and tried to muster the energy it would take to make it through the night. I knew he would want sex and that was the last thing I wanted. Maybe he would have to make a quick drug run. Maybe a crack head would rap on the door and irritate him by begging for some shake and then maybe he'd forget about sex for the night. Maybe. Hopefully. I drug myself into the bedroom and hung the wet towel I'd used to dry off with evenly across the top of the door as I had been taught to do. Prevent, prevent, prevent. I put on a full set of pajamas. He'll have to work a little harder and maybe he won't feel like working. Another long ass sigh and I climb into bed. He's already in bed. Waiting for me no doubt. I'd also learned to read the energy in the room and tonight it was settled. Not violent or disruptive. Not peaceful either, just settled. He turned to me and said, "You knew didn't you?" Awwww hell, here we go again.

"Knew what?"

"You knew I had already taken all the Doritos out of that pack. You just didn't want to tell me that I didn't have any more Doritos. You thought that shit was funny. Why didn't you just tell me I didn't have any more Doritos?"

This is the thing about crazy: you can't reason with it and you must not respond to it from a rational place because you will drive yourself insane doing so.

"I don't know Marvin." Lawd let this idiot take this answer and go to sleep. Please Jesus!

And just as I suspected he starts trying to put his hand down my pajama pants. Another long sigh. This is going to be a theme for the night. Lots of long sighs. At that point I was still allowed to do that. He is breathing on my neck and moving his hand further and further down my pants. His breath is making me sick. I wish it would just stop. All of it. But, it doesn't and soon he's barking out orders as usual. "Open your legs, dang! Let me get in." I did as I was told. As I wandered off mentally thinking about what I needed to do the next day, he humped away oblivious to the fact that I was not even in the same room with him. I'm sure he didn't care or maybe he really didn't know. I'd gotten pretty good at making the appropriate sounds at the appropriate times. Oochie ouch muthafucker!

Whatever you need to hurry this thing along is fine with me. Prevent, prevent, prevent. A little while later another order is barked at me, "Turn over. Hurry up while it's still hard, damn! You so slow with the shit. And can you throw it back this time? Shit!" Yeah this is how we 'had sex.' Soon enough he'd finish. And eventually he did. He finished and rolled over. If this ain't some Ceily shit, I don't know what is. This shit is crazy.

I will say one thing: I had to be young and dumb because I used to sleep like a rock around this deranged fool. I was sound asleep in the bed of the enemy without a second thought. I can't imagine doing something that dangerous now. I had become so used to him getting out of bed after slight knocks on the door and windows from dirty crack heads that I didn't even really wake up anymore. I would shift in my sleep, but I wasn't too bothered at all by it. I got my zzz's in. Tonight was no different. I was sound asleep and quite cozy in my PJ's. I was trying to roll over and something was in my way. I struggled a little in my sleep and slowly I woke up because I really couldn't turn over. When I opened my eyes all I could see was Marvin on top of me. He was closer than close. His eyes were right at my eyes and he was staring at me. His lips were right at my lips and I could feel the air from his lungs each time he exhaled. He wasn't saying anything. I was lying on my back and I could feel his forearm across my chest pressing down on me. The rest of his body weight was also pressing down on me. He had one leg between my legs and his hips were on top of mine. That's why I couldn't move. His weight had me pinned to the bed.

Who knows how long he'd been on top of me like this. Staring. Waiting for me to wake up. Even if I'd wanted to jump from being startled, I couldn't. My entire body was pinned. I tried to move the arm that was not pinned under his body and I felt the grip he had on my wrist tighten. He'd thought of everything and I was powerless. He probably had an erection from that thought alone. "What are you doing?" His lips were so close to mine I could barely speak. He moved his leg from between my legs and brought his knee up to my wrist. He moved the hand that was holding my wrist and replaced it with his knee. He pressed it down onto my wrist and into the mattress. All while still staring into my eyes. Then he shifted his hips further over on top of me so that he was lying directly on top of me with his body parallel to mine and his knee pressed into my wrist. He was pressing down on me with so much force it was getting hard for me to breathe. Once he was sure I was bound, he moved his forearm from my chest. I gulped and inhaled deeply to fill my lungs with air. Before I could exhale he began to speak.

"You think you're slick. But I know what you do when you think I don't know. When you think I'm not looking, I know what you are doing."

"I'm not doing….." my voice trailed off.

"If you even *dream* about another nigga I will kill your ass! If you even *think* about leaving me I will make you miserable. I – will – fuck – you – up!"

He had threatened me countless times before, but never like this. This was really, really scary. He didn't usually bother me at night or especially so soon after I 'gave him some.' He had never pinned me down like that. At least not while I was sleeping, anyway. And he had never pulled a weapon on me before. I felt the coldness of the blade against my neck before I felt the sharpness of it. The fear that I felt that night was palpable and it's impossible to put into words what it feels like to know that someone is capable of killing you. And that they WILL kill you. It is a feeling that is so life altering that anyone who experiences it is surely a different person afterwards. The way you view the world is forever changed. I was a different person after that night.

I was scared to swallow. I thought he'd surely cut me if I moved. The blade of the knife was pressed against my throat and I was unsure if swallowing would cause me to be cut. He slowly rolled over and got out of the bed. He went into the kitchen and I heard him put the knife back into the drawer. He walked calmly back to bed and turned his back to me. His short breaths slowly became deeper and deeper and I listened to him fall asleep. 20 minutes or more must have passed but I had not moved. Not a muscle. I'm surprised I was able to breathe while lying that still. I didn't sleep that night, but at some point I did muster the courage to roll over onto my side and exhale. This is something way bigger than had I thought before. That night was the first time I realized I was in over my head. Way over my head. I wasn't equipped by any stretch of the imagination to deal with what was taking place under that roof. That night I learned what living in a state of sustained fear felt like. All I could think was - *how am I going to get out of this*? From that night forward, my thoughts were consumed by fear, survival and escape.

I was working at the front desk of a hotel and going to school. I could only take one class at a time and keep him at arm's length, so for now, that would have to do. While I was at work I would constantly think about how I could get away from him. I'd think about what I would need when I made the move and the first thing that came to mind was always money. I would need money to leave. Literally. I had no car so I would have to call a cab. I didn't want my friends to know everything that was going on and most of them had gone off to college and weren't in town at the time anyway. I'd need money to get my own place. I might need money to get out of the lease at the place we were renting. Any which way I looked at it, the cash flow had to happen. I worked and worked and worked. And I squirreled away all that money. For the most part he was paying the household bills. I paid a utility bill here or there and I bought groceries (yes those damn Doritos too!) and I was responsible for all the gas for the car we shared. He had reasoned that since I wanted to go to school and work I should be made to pay for the gas that would otherwise not have been needed. Go figure. Whatever. I was compliant. This was phase one of the plan I was developing. It was an escape plan and I needed it to be fool proof. The problem was that I was so young and inexperienced I didn't even know all the things I needed to plan for. I kept going with what I knew and what I had.

Phase 2 of the plan came to me one day at work. I was talking to an older gentleman who worked nearby and he said something to me that sparked an idea in my mind. He was talking about some guests in his establishment who had been complaining about the service they'd received. He wasn't angry and he had accommodated them to the best of his ability. He said that even after he had complied with all their requests, they were still hostile. He came to the conclusion that these people only wanted to be told that they were right. Right in complaining, right in being displeased with the service, right in remaining hostile after the situation had been rectified. He said, "People just want to be right. And even if they're wrong, they want you to tell them that they're right."

For whatever reason that philosophy stuck with me. I put it in my back pocket and took it home with me. And let me tell you, that thang worked like a charm! See, my focus at that time was survival. The way to survive with Messy Marvin was to not wake the sleeping bear. If I could keep him placated I could buy myself some time.

By then I knew I was in a fight to stay alive. Every time I had an encounter with him I could be physically hurt. That was what I thought. I never thought I would actually die. I knew he was capable of killing me. I knew that for a fact, but inside myself somewhere I knew that my fate would not be to die at his hands. Now I'm a bit vain too, and I didn't want to leave the relationship alive with a limp either, so survival mode was in full effect. Everything he asked or demanded of me, I did. No questions asked. Everything he said, I agreed with. I told him he was right in so many different ways he became suspicious of his own 'rightness.' I would find him questioning himself after I had already agreed with him. He would make a statement; I would agree – "Yep. Sure is!; he would turn to me and ask, "Are you sure I got that right?"; I would reiterate – "Yep! Sure is! This went on for weeks and weeks. But I had a master plan in place and I really felt it was working.

One day he came in the house and slammed the door behind him. Oh shit! He was in that crazy mood. He walked around slamming and bamming things around. He showered from work, changed clothes, ate dinner and had his ice cream – ALL in silence. Not a single word. My heart was beating so damn fast and hard I just *knew* he heard it. I made sure to steer clear. While he showered, I went outside and sat on the porch. When he ate dinner I sat in the living room and read a book. While he sat on the sofa and ate his ice cream I sat on the love seat and looked straight ahead at the TV, making sure he had the remote control at his fingertips and that the TV was turned to his favorite channel.

While he was eating his ice cream he asked me why I wasn't having any. I promptly ran my black ass to the kitchen and fixed myself a bowl of ice cream. You know how Ceily ran outta that kitchen and left the chair rocking when Mister went to light the stove? Yeah, that love seat was looking like Ceily's rocker because that's how fast I got up and made my way to the kitchen to fix that bowl of ice cream. While I sat there eating ice cream he asked what I was doing the next day. Odd, to say the least. "Nothing much. I get off work at 3 tomorrow."

"We going to my mama's house tomorrow when I pick you up from work."

"We are?"

"Yeah, damn! Don't start asking me a million fucking questions either. We just going. That's all you need to know."

That ain't hardly all I need to know, but I was ♪ thinkin' of a master plan ♫. "Ok. I'll be ready when you pick me up."

"Go take a shower so I can hit that tonight." This was the hardest part of the damn plan. By now he repulsed me and the thought of him on top of me was not something I welcomed. We hadn't even talked about that incident with the knife, but I had noticed that every time he would get on top of me I'd feel this incredible fear flow through me. I always felt suffocated in that bed with him now. I'm gonna be fucked up whenever I *do* get out of this crazy ass relationship. I know that for sure.

Sure enough, the next day he pulls up in front of where I worked at 2:59 p.m. At 3:02 p.m. we were on our way to his mom's house. I had never really heard him talk about her much. Another sign ladies. If you're dating a man, especially a black man, and he never mentions his mother, something is definitely awry. I think he had mentioned that she 'lived across town' and that she was 'crazy from working all these years.' But other than that, I hadn't heard much else about her. When we drove into the neighborhood, I realized that it was familiar to me. I had been to this part of town before. One of my mom's friends lived just down the street. He slowly pulled the car into the driveway. It was a semi-circular driveway and there was a Chevy Cavalier parked halfway under the car port. You could tell the yard had been what you would consider 'nice' at some point, but that day it looked unkempt.

It had recently rained and all the leaves that hadn't been removed from the last time the lawn was done were wet and muddy and embedded in the grass. The stone of the fountain on the front lawn was stained green and the water inside the fountain was black and muddy and full of debris. The rain water had splashed from inside the fountain up onto the cherub that stood in the muddy water and black dirty spots were all over its face and body. It looked sad. Even the pavement on the driveway was dirty. Kinda gross. But I could tell it wasn't always this way. I didn't grow up like this. Our lawn was always manicured to a Tee. The hedges were always clipped perfectly and the leaves were definitely not ever left on the lawn to be rained on. I have no idea what I'm getting ready to walk into.

He's at the front door walking into the house before I can get the car door open. Geesh! Typical. I jump out, skip and hop my happy self up to the door in a poor attempt to catch up with him. BAM! The door slams in my face just as I get close. Rude bastard. I hear him screaming inside the same way he does in our apartment. "Ma! Where you at? I'm hungry. You ain't cook?" By now I'm inside trying to find my way to where he is by following the sound of his voice. The house looks like 1978. You know that time frame right before the 80's when the Foxy Brown/Shaft era was over but the Miami Vice era wasn't here yet? Yeah, that's what it looked like. There was a wall that was brick – inside the damn house? – then there was a wall of paneling on the opposite side of the room. I think I saw a fireplace and some green carpet in the blur as I was rushing to find Marvin. You can't have me just lost wandering around your mom's house. What if I bump into her before I find you in here? She doesn't even know I'm with you or who I am. After rounding the bend into 1985 I find dude sitting at a full out bar.

With an overhang full of wine glasses, stuffed leather countertop and barstools to match. He's sitting there waiting for her to come bring him some food, I guess. I climb up on the stool next to him and wait too. Soon I hear a voice far off say, "I'm on my way in there." Hmmm, she sounds....normal. Actually, nice. I didn't know what to expect, but it wasn't normal. How could normal create this kind of crazy? Stay open, stay open. Damn, I'm talking to myself now. His crazy is rubbing off on me. Lord help me.

She walks in and I hate to say it, but she did look like *something* had driven her crazy. LMAO! I don't know if it was working too much that did it, but something ain't right here. I feel bad that I'm finding humor in this, but this shit is hilarious. She looks like a bumbling, absent minded professor. Her glasses are askew on her face, her hair is in a bun that is a lil lop sided on top of her head and she looks lost in her own house. This is going to be a circus. Barnum & Bailey and the damn Ringling Brothers all rolled up into one lady. She came in and after tripping over her own feet she asks him what he wants and starts listing off what she has that she can heat up for him.

"Just make me a grilled cheese Daisy. Damn!" He just called him mama by her first name! She gon' snap, she gon' snap. Oh shit! She didn't snap...huh? She has pulled a plate out and started to pile on leftovers to heat up for him, when she looks over in surprise – "Oh heeeey!" How you doing?" What. The. Hell. "Did you bring her in here with you Marvin?" He gets up, grabs his crotch and says,

"Shut up Daisy! You crazy as hell." I don't even know how to process what is going on. Who calls their mom by her first name? Who commands her around her own house like this? Who tells their mama to shut up? I just can't with these two right now. So I try to step in with something rational.

"Yes ma'am I came with him."

"Ha Ha Ha! I didn't even *see* you. You want something to eat too?"

"No ma'am I'm ok." I was not about to eat anything in this house.

"Marvin, why she keep calling me 'ma'am'?"

"That's the type shit she do. Just fix my plate. That's why I didn't even want to bring her over here."

"Oh ok. You want me to fix your plate?"

"You are so crazy, ma, damn! You already got it on the plate."

Now even though this is funny as hell, I'm starting to feel bad for her. There is obviously something wrong. I'm thinking she shouldn't be living alone. I don't think it's safe for her to go unattended. Seriously.

She made the plate, he ate and we left. That was it. I didn't say another word to her and her, not another word to me. I did watch, though. A lot. They had a strange dynamic, to say the least, but I could see that there was some type of bond between them. He had always avoided direct eye contact, even with me (sign number 973! I know!) but when she tried to touch him or hug him as we rose to leave, he seemed even more uncomfortable than usual. He swayed his head side to side when she tried to force him to look her in the face. She even grabbed both sides of his face with her hands in an attempt to steady his head. He closed his eyes. There is something very wrong with this man. Very wrong.

We got in the car and headed toward the apartment. While we drove I looked out of the window and I thought. What the hell has gone on in that house and in his life to fuck him up like this? What has happened to that poor woman we just left unattended? Who did this to them? For some reason I didn't think she was the one who fucked him up. She didn't seem to have it in her. Then it hit me.

My mom had told me something when I first met him. He'd come to pick me up one day and she saw him as he stood in the doorway, completely uncomfortable, waiting for me. When I got back home she asked me what his name was. I told her and as soon as I got the name out of my mouth she said, "Yeah, that's what I thought. He's a fool. So is his mama. The whole family is crazy. I know that for a fact. His dad beat his mama so bad. That's all they do in that family is fight. I can't believe they're all still living." I blew it off because, for the most part, my mom never liked anyone I dated. I honestly had not thought about it since she said that. Not until now.

Chapter 3

Back at the ranch things pretty much stayed the
same. I kept yessing him and he kept being crazy as hell.
I had reached the point where I was positive that the very
next episode of the Crazy Show would be the finale. I
was leaving. This was too much for me. I had some
money saved, but still not the amount I felt I needed to
leave and stand alone. I had finished a few semesters, but
still no degree. I had decided to leave, but I still had no
real solid plan. At this time it didn't matter anymore. I
couldn't sleep well, I was constantly walking on egg
shells and keeping the sleeping bear snoozing was just
getting to be a real pain in the ass. I had somewhat of a
timetable because I knew as soon as I stopped agreeing
with everything he said I'd have a fight on my hands.

Sure enough the time came one night not long
after I had made up my mind. He was in a mood from
earlier in the afternoon. Hard day of picking up cones I
guess. The afternoon made its way into the evening and
his mood stayed the same. No better, no worse. He was
doing his usual crazy-ass-man-on-the-corner pacing, back
and forth; his slamming and bamming; his cursing aloud,
but tonight he was talking to himself too. Kinda under his
breath, but kinda not. It was loud enough for me to hear
him, but I couldn't always make out every word. It was
like loud, mad mumbling. I was still doing the Ceily and
steering clear. I had already showered and had everything
ready for work the next day. I was sitting in the front of
the apartment eating my ice cream, watching T.V. and
listening to the rain outside. It was pouring. The banging
and talking became louder and louder over the next 30

minutes or so. A few weeks earlier he had decided he needed a bike for several reasons I didn't really care about. Because of this there was a 10 speed bicycle that had been housed in the dining area of the apartment for at least 3 weeks. It was parked on the side of the table we didn't normally use. When he'd had enough of the one-way conversation, he came into the front where I was and flopped himself down on the sofa.

"Fuck you looking over here for? Ain't shit over here for you to see." So not in the mood for this bullshit tonight. I got up, without responding, and walked into the kitchen to put my bowl away. Here he comes. Loud, trying to start a fight and just looking for it. I tried to walk out of the kitchen, but he blocked my way at the door.

"You think you just gon' ignore me? Like I ain't even here?"

"I'm not ignoring you. Can you please move so I can go to bed? I'm tired." Of course he just stands there. Staring me down. I tried to leave again and he moved in front of me. I moved to the left, he moved to the left. I moved to the right, he moved to the right. I let out a giant sigh and took a few steps backwards. It was now no longer ok to sigh around him.

"Oh you got a problem? What? What? What's the problem? You wanna leave the kitchen? Make me move then since you so fucking frustrated." By now he's up in my face and my back is against the refrigerator.

"No. I don't have a problem. I'm just sleepy, that's all." Prevent, prevent, prevent. This prevention thing is truly difficult sometimes. I want to knock his ass outta my way. For real.

"Nah, you ain't sleepy. You think you can just do whatever the fuck you wanna do. That's what it is." He's very close to my face and he's talking through his clinched teeth. I know this is a big one and I may not be able to get out of it easily tonight. Damn it! I had learned to not look him in the eye so I was looking down at my feet. I put both hands up to my chest and kept my head down. I wanted to take a step to the left and try to go around him, but crazy is not rational. And crazy never will be rational.

Before my foot could touch the ground from attempting to make that side step I felt the heat across my face from his hand. It was an open handed slap and it knocked my head back into the refrigerator. It stung so bad. It stung, hurt and burned all at the same time. The entire left side of my face was hot. It burned like crazy. I don't know about others, but my mind tends to work extremely fast when I'm in crisis mode. I think very clearly. I believe most people panic and they don't think. In my mind, things slow down and become crystal clear. My focus is laser sharp and I can avoid or exit a situation faster than normal. When my head bounced off the refrigerator door I kept my eyes down and I let my head hang low.

You see, when he's in kill mode, Marvin is a predator. Most predators pounce when they notice that their prey is vulnerable. I knew he'd step into me when he saw that I hung my head and didn't look up at him. He took that as his opportunity to fully overtake me. Kill mode also heightens bravado and so the predator doesn't see his own weakness or vulnerability. His ego is in FULL control of his actions. In learning to survive I had watched and analyzed and I knew what his weaknesses were. As soon as he stepped in I ducked and gut punched that ass as hard as I could. He was thin and he folded in half. I had to take that left step after all to prevent his head from hitting me. He banged his head against the refrigerator. BAM! I tried to run, but he turned quickly and grabbed my shirt. It was a tug of war. Me trying to run out of the kitchen and him pulling me by my shirt back toward him. I twisted my body and my shirt slipped out of his hand. By then he'd recovered and was chasing me. He quickly caught me and spun me around so that I was facing him. He tried to choke me but I grabbed his hand and pushed against it as hard as I could. He was pushing his hand down hard trying to get it around my neck.

I couldn't let him get his hands around my neck. He would surely choke me to death if he did. He was pushing down and I was pushing up. He overpowered me and his hand slammed against my face. His fingers were near my eyes and he was trying to slide his hand down my face. Damn! He's still trying to get his hand around my neck. By now I had grabbed his forearm and I was pulling it up and trying to push it away from my face. He was bearing down hard and his hand was sliding down my face. I couldn't over power him. He was simply stronger than I was. I would have to outsmart him if I wanted to get away.

I let go of his forearm and when his hand cupped my chin I opened my mouth. His fingers fell inside and I clamped my teeth down like a pit-bull! He grimaced in pain and tried to force my mouth open with his other hand. I was holding on for dear life. I didn't know what he'd do if he got both hands free now! I was so afraid. He was clawing at my face with his free hand. There were fingers in my nostrils and my eyes, but I wouldn't let go. Screw that I've got to keep him trapped! Suddenly he stopped clawing at my face. He bent his body down and grabbed me around my waist and started pushing me back. What the hell? Was he trying to run me into the wall? What is he doing?

I was now stammering to stay upright. I was running backwards. His momentum was pushing me backwards faster and faster. He lifted his head and we were almost eye to eye. I felt a sharp pain in my back and I screamed in agony, "Aghhhhh!" It felt like I had been stabbed. Whatever had just stuck me in the back was sharp and metal. Then I heard a loud crash and we both tumbled to the ground on top of that stupid bicycle. The handle bar had hit me in the back. We had crashed to the floor and I had landed on top of the pedal. I could tell my back was bleeding. The pedal had slid across my back and cut me open. I was squirming beneath him trying to find my footing. He was struggling too, but he was on top of me. I was moving really quick and he was trying to pin me down, but the bike was also moving and the wheels were spinning and neither one of us could balance enough to stand. I managed to turn over so that I could try to use my hands against the floor to push my body up.

"Aghhhhhh" I screamed out again. This son of a bitch bit me. He had clamped onto the back of my shoulder with his teeth. He was biting into my flesh hard! "Aghhhh fuck!!" I screamed again. I stopped trying to get up and I let my body fall on top of the bike. He was up in a flash when he saw that I'd given up. He grabbed my arm and turned me over onto my back and started in.

He was punching, kicking and slapping me and then he pulled me completely off the bike and threw me onto the floor on my back. He bent down over me and put both hands around my neck. Damn, I cannot die like this. I can't breathe anymore. I have no air left in my lungs. He was bearing down on my chest with his knee and I felt so weak. I couldn't fight against him anymore. My hands fell from the grip I had on his forearms and I felt my eyes close. Everything went black.

When I opened my eyes I was gasping for breath. Marvin was straddling me. He had one knee on the floor on either side of my body. He had his hands propped on his hips and he was breathing heavily looking down at me. My throat was hurting. I'm not sure if it hurt from the screaming or the choking. He was just sitting there like he was cooling off from a jog or something. I tried to wiggle my toes. Check. Tried to move my arms. Check. Blinked my eyes a few times. Check. Then I swallowed, slowly. Check. Ok. I'm still alive. I have to get THEE fuck outta this house **TONIGHT!**

I shifted my weight up onto my elbows with my forearms flat on the floor. My head was tucked and my chin was touching my chest. "Can you get off me?" I said it calmly and very slowly. He didn't say a word in response, but he lifted himself up off me. I got up. My head was spinning and I was definitely dizzy. He stood nearby. Watching. He was still trying to catch his breath. I walked pass him and went into the bedroom. My mind was moving much faster than my body was. I had to leave. Now, right now. This had gotten to be entirely too much for me to bare. I found a suitcase in the closet up high on a shelf and I started to fold my clothes and put them into the suitcase. When I finished there I gathered my shoes and put them into a duffle bag I pulled from under the bed. When I had everything together I sat on the edge of the bed. I reached over to the nightstand beside the bed and took the phone off the receiver. I dialed the numbers and listened while it rang… "Yes, I need a cab, please."

"Address." A dry, matter-of-fact voice barked back at me. I gave the address and waited. "Somebody'll be there in 15 minutes." A dial tone was what I heard next. I just sat there with the phone in my hand. Dazed. I honestly didn't know how I was going to make it the short distance from the bedroom to the front door, down the stairs and into a waiting cab, without him killing me somewhere along the way. If I had to I'd leave the suitcase and duffle bag and just run. I could probably get halfway without him trying to stop me if he didn't see anything in my hands. If I emerged from the bedroom with packed bags he would surely flip the fuck out and I would be back on the floor unconscious by the time the cab arrived. The beeping of the receiver in my lap snapped me out of my fog. I hung the phone up. Oddly, he hadn't come looking for me. I was sure he'd walk into the bedroom, but I hadn't heard a sound from him. I sat there deep in thought until I came up with a plan. I would wait until the cab was downstairs to walk out with my packed bags. That's my best hope. I slid the suitcase and the duffle bag under the edge of the bed and looked over at the digital clock on the nightstand. I had about 10 more minutes.

Beep! Beep! It was the cab. My heart was thumping inside my chest. Superbass! Game time, let's go! I got up and reached under the bed. I pulled out the suitcase and duffle bag and walked into the living room with them both. I sat them down at the dining room table where he was sitting. I was so anxious. I just wanted to be outside in the cab. If I'd had a little wiggly nose and some T.V. magic, I would have been in business. He was looking straight ahead starring at the wall. I walked in, in front of the luggage (in case I had to haul ass) and said "Marvin, I'm leaving. I can't take this and I don't want to live here with you like this anymore. I'm gonna go. That's my ride downstairs." He turned his head in my direction and looked at me. "You're leaving? Tonight? Right now? You don't want to talk first?"

"I don't want to talk. I just want to leave. I wanna go."

"You playin' right?"

"I'm for real. I gotta go before my ride leaves, ok?" As crazy as it sounds, somewhere inside of me I wanted him to be ok with me leaving. I think that would have made me feel less insane. It would've meant that he knew how fucked up he had been to me and that he understood why I wanted to leave.

"Let's tell your ride you're not leaving. Then you can unpack all that stuff and we will just talk about how you can not piss me off the way you do." He was freakishly calm. He spoke in a normal tone and he was still seated. My insides were screaming, run, run, run! I knew this was an opportunity and I took it. I turned and picked up my bags and made my way to the door before he got up.

"Wait a minute! You can't just leave without saying anything to me." There is something different about his voice. He isn't yelling at me. He's loud, but not yelling. I had never heard him sound like this before. He was actually...pleading...with me. He wanted me to stay. That was clear, but his voice wasn't threatening. In that moment he was making a request. That was completely unfamiliar to me. He'd never *asked* me anything since the

40

day we met. Everything had always been a command. His tone shocked me so much that I turned to look at him as I opened the front door. Mama didn't raise no fool. I was still tryna get the hell up outta there. I was searching his face for a sign of deceit. This had to be a trick to get me to stay so he could kill me. There was no way this man did not want to finish what he'd started tonight. I looked him in his eyes and I searched his face. Strange. All I saw was sadness. I stared for a minute. The only emotion I had ever witnessed from him was anger. I didn't know what to make of it. I kept staring. I saw a glimpse of his mother in his face. BEEP! BEEP! The cab driver blew the horn again. I jumped. I pushed the door all the way open and stepped out onto the concrete.

The rain was coming down in sheets. It was so loud outside. I drug the suitcase across the threshold. I had the duffle bag on my shoulder already. My shirt was stuck to my shoulder from the dried blood underneath. I felt it but I kept moving. He came out onto the slab of concrete too. I started to take the stairs. One at a time. Carefully. I was in enough physical pain. I didn't want to fall down the concrete stairs in the rain and die trying to escape this lunatic.

He stood at the doorway screaming my name. He was pleading now. "Please! Please! Come back in the house. Where are you going? You can't be for real! Please come back. Wait, wait, wait. Don't leave!" By then I was humping it down those stairs. The cab driver had seen me coming and had backed the cab up so that it was closer to the bottom of the staircase. Not that it helped any. The rain was insane and I was already pretty wet. I didn't look back and I kept taking the stairs one at a time. Damn this duffle bag is heavy as shit and my back stung all over now. The bite mark was on fire from the wet shirt and the duffle bag rubbed against it every time I took a step down. The long cut from the bike pedal was agonizing with that wet shirt stuck to it, but I had finally reached the last step. I couldn't stop now. My heart was beating so fast and I was scared to death. I didn't know what I was going to do once I left that apartment, but I couldn't go back now that I'd made it out. I sat the suitcase down on the ground and the water splashed up to my thighs. There had to be 4 inches of water on the ground. I grabbed the door of the cab and the handle slipped right out of my hand. I was so nervous that my hand was shaking. I reached for the door handle again and I felt him behind me. I still didn't look back.

I managed to get the door open. I threw the duffle bag inside and I saw the cab driver look over his shoulder at me. Ummm, no sir, I don't need any help AT ALL! Jerk! You see me out here struggling with this rain pounding on me. Marvin was behind me screaming at the top of his lungs now. I could hear his voice over the sound of the rain. I wasn't going to look back. I was too afraid. I stepped one foot inside the cab and that's when I felt him grab me. He had a hold of my leg that was still outside the cab. He wrapped himself around my thigh. I was trying to shake him off me. I still hadn't looked back at him. I laid down in the back seat of the cab and put all the weight of my body on the seat as I tried again to shake my leg loose from his grip.

Everything was so wet. There was water everywhere. I grabbed the inside door handle and held on. I was trying to pull myself inside the cab so I could close the door. My suitcase was still outside, but I really didn't care. It would just have to be left. As I kicked him with my free leg he slid down my thigh. Dammit, he just won't let go! He has my calf and my ankle now. I was pulling myself up in the seat to try to get some balance and leverage so that I can kick him harder. Anything to get him off me. I slid helplessly across the seat from his weight pulling on my leg, from the water and from pure exhaustion. The only thing I could do was stand up. I put my weight on the foot that he was holding onto and I held on to the top of the cab and the door with my body still inside. I am NOT getting out of this cab now. In the meantime the damn cab driver was enjoying the show. He had done a complete 180 in the driver's seat and was just watching all wide eyed and what not.

I stood up I looked down at Marvin. He was clinging to my ankle for dear life. He was on his knees, there in the rain, like a child. He was shaking. As I looked down on him I saw that he was weeping. Like a baby. Not even what I'd call crying. He was weeping. And he was begging. Pleading with me. "Please, please, please stay. Please don't leave me. Don't leave me here by myself. Please, don't go. Please, don't go. I don't want you to leave me. Please, stay. Don't leave. It will be better. I'll do better. Just please don't leave me here by myself like this. I don't know what to do. Please stay."

For the first time since he struck me back in my mother's house, I was not afraid. I didn't feel fear. I felt for him. I felt some sort of empathy for him. I didn't see the monster that had terrorized my life. I didn't see the violent, abuser who had lashed out at me and struck me time and time again. I didn't see the controlling, threatening beast I had lived with. I didn't see the person I lived with in that apartment just a few feet away. When I looked down at him I saw who he really, truly was. I saw a wounded soul. A very sad, sad, sad being. A hurt and helpless child. A lost man. I had no clue how to process that. It did not fit with any idea, thought, memory or knowledge I had about this person. I literally didn't know what to do with what I felt and saw in that moment. He needed … something. Help me Jesus (and all 12 disciples)! What the hell was going on here? Oh my God. What was I going to do?

I dropped the suitcase on the ground. I didn't even realize I'd been holding onto the handle that whole time. The water splashed on his face and onto my leg. This damn cabbie! He opens his door and pokes his head out so that he can get a better look at dude down here on the ground crying and begging and probably slobbering too, but the rain took care of that. I have to make a decision here. My heart is aching and racing all at the same damn time. I can't quiet it enough to think. I stepped my other foot outside the cab and closed the door. The cab driver's gaze quickly snapped up at my face with a huge question mark. His mouth hung open. I shook my head side to side and he mouthed a silent ok. Leaning up against the door of the cab, I just let the rain soak me more than it already had.

44

With my arms across my chest, "Get up!" I was yelling at him over the sound of the rain. "Get up!" Again to be sure he heard me. He didn't get up, but he let go of my leg. It throbbed. Man, he had been holding on tight. He just stayed there. Squatting down on the ground with his head hung low. "Do you hear me?" I yelled again. He shook his head, yes. "I am leaving tonight." He reached out to grab my leg again and I pulled them apart so that he couldn't touch me. "I AM LEAVING! You treat me like shit and I'm sick of living here with you like this! You're fucked up. Really fucked up. And I can't help you." I was scared as shit saying that to him. I had no idea how he might react. I needed to say it though. I had been holding it in for so long I had to let it out. I felt terrible. Like I wanted to throw up, but I had to keep moving. Mentally I had to keep moving or I'd be frozen. I felt for him. I did. My heart broke when I saw him exposed and vulnerable and begging me to stay. Naturally my instinct was to reach out and offer help or to ease his pain. Even though it was a person who had caused me so much pain. But I have to put that aside right now. I did not want to end up like those women you see 20 years after the day they should have left. They look haggard in the face, shoulders look like they've been carrying the weight of the world, eyes all sunken in and dreams snatched. Nah, that won't be me. I've got too much to end up like that. I gotta go.

I picked up the suitcase and opened the cab door again. I had to wedge myself in because he hadn't moved. I sat the suitcase on the floorboard and closed the door. "Lock the doors. This nigga is crazy." To which the cab driver promptly slammed his hand down on the lock button. CLICK! "Just leave. Drive. Drive before he gets up." He hit the gas and in a few seconds we were turning out of the complex. I cried the entire way home.

Chapter 4

After a few days of relaxation I felt better. My back had healed a bit and my mind was clearing up. I felt better. I had missed a couple days of work and school, but I wasn't too concerned about either. I could easily catch up at school and work was, well, work. The place still ran without me. My mother on the other hand was completely over Mr. Messy. He had been calling non-stop since the night I left him. It was pure insanity. He called 24-7. Eventually, my mom just took the phone completely off the hook and left it off. If either of us placed the phone back on the receiver it would ring immediately.

He was crazed, for sure. He had to be just sitting there dialing repeatedly. Who does that? At one point my mom turned to me and asked me, "What is wrong with him? Seriously. How were you able to live with this?" I just looked at her puzzled. I did not have the answer. I had been asking myself that since I left him. What *is* wrong with him? The image of him down on the ground in the rain, begging like that had stayed with me. How could the monster I'd come to know reside in the same mind and body of that wounded man?

It just did not compute for me. I tossed the question around in my mind often and I was always stumped. I don't know how that happens, but something had fractured him. He'd been split into two. My mom was ready to call the cops and have his ass committed. Maybe the professionals could figure it out. I don't know.

Day 4 of this non-stop nonsense and I felt I had to at least talk to him. I mean, maybe he just wanted to say what he had to say. Who knew? I just knew it had to stop. I was not going back to that hell hole to live with him and I was about to be evicted from my mother's house because of his shenanigans. I had to do something. I picked up the phone and placed it down onto the receiver. RING! RING! RING! Within 5 seconds he was on the other end. "What do you want Marvin? You are driving my mom insane. You can't do this! What?! What do you want?"

"Why won't you just talk to me? All you had to do all this time was just answer the phone."

"Ok. Now I'm on the phone. What do you want?"

"Can you just come outside and talk to me? If…"

"Outside! Where are you?"

"If I come over there. Will you come outside and talk to me?"

"Why can't you just say what you have to say on the phone now? My mom is going to go crazy if she sees you in her driveway. You can't come over here. I came here when I left the apartment so she knows I wasn't happy over there. She knows it ain't good between us. You can't come here. My mom is not going for that. AT ALL! She will call the cops."

"Well walk down the street and meet me." Do you see how crazy does? Crazy is not rational in any way. You have attacked me, beat me, verbally abused me, chocked me out, held a knife to my throat and now you want me to be in cahoots with you to fool my own damn mama. My only safety net. The person I ran to in order to get away from your crazy ass. Lord help this child.

"I'm not doing that. Say whatever you gotta say now so you can stop calling here."

"Man! Why you can't just come down the street? It ain't like I'm asking for a whole lot. Damn!"

"I'm not coming down the street. I'm not moving back in with you. I'm not doing any of that. Tell me what you want to tell me now. You're not gonna get me alone and choke the shit outta me again. You have a real anger problem and I'm not tryna do that today with you. What do you want to say that you can't just say now?" Now a person better equipped to manage crazy would probably have just hung up, called the police, obtained a restraining order and fled the city, but again, I was young and dumb and my mind was messed up then. I wanted him to say something to make it all make sense to me.

Your mind is always hoping for that moment of clarity from them. You want him to say or do something to redeem himself and make it all ok. Something that makes sense so you yourself don't feel like you're loosing it. It's almost as if what's happening to you is so out there you want him to give you that golden nugget so you understand your own reactions to the whole thing. You don't know why you stay either. You don't know why you didn't leave the first time. You don't know why you ever thought it would get any better. You don't know why you care about what happens to someone who hurts you. You don't know why you are even on the phone with this fool.

"Please. I just wanna talk to you face to face. I know I'm fucked up. I ain't gonna hit you. I promise I won't. I'm calm now. I just wanna talk to you and explain why I did that. Explain what happened. Just come down the street. Please. Please." His voice was trailing off. That other side was showing itself. The vulnerable side. Damn! Why do I feel bad? I didn't cause this. I shouldn't care. This dude has put his hands on me. I should want him hung by a noose. Instead I'm actually considering meeting with him to hear what he has to say. It's the "explain what happened" that I think got me. I wanna know what happened too.

How the hell can chips, and good morning greetings and wanting to go to bed make you attack a person? Not just any person, but me. Make you attack me? What is that? Maybe he knows himself and he really does know what makes him act that way. Maybe if I just listen to him. That can't hurt, right? This is the mind wrestling that goes on.

I pulled a hooded sweatshirt over my head and it snagged the new scab that had formed over the bite on my shoulder. I ignored it and quickly threw on a pair of sweatpants. I grabbed a pair of slides and I walked out of the front door without saying a word to anyone. I walked down the driveway away from the safety of my mother's house and walked onto the sidewalk toward his car. He was parked at the end of the street. I was thinking to myself. *What is he going to say?* My mind still had hope.

50

I was hopeful he would say that *something* that I needed to hear to make it all make sense. But I really had no idea what might happen. I was so confused. I didn't even know why I had agreed to see him. I had pulled the hoodie over my head. The shame had reared its ugly head. As I approached the car, my heart began to race. I didn't know what it was, but looking back at the situation now, my body and mind knew that I was in danger. My body was responding to what my mind had grown numb to. This was not a safe place to be, physically. I opened the car door and sat inside. He turned the key and my heart almost jumped out of my chest.

Was he going to kidnap me? Holy shit! This was a bad idea. "Where are you going?" I blurted it out before I really wanted to. I was trying to play it cool. I was still in my neighborhood and I could get out if I needed to. "We don't need to leave. Turn the car off." I had to recover from that weak sounding first question I'd blurted out. He looked over at me with an evil eye. "I'm not playing. I will get out and walk back home." I opened the car door. He reached up and turned the car off without taking his eyes off me. "What do you want? You had so much to say on the phone that you needed to see me in person. Go ahead."

"You don't miss me? You don't want to come back?"

"No. I don't want to come back. I don't want to live with you anymore. You are too mean. I don't like it and I can't take you hitting me Marvin. That shit ain't right. I've never been hit in my whole life."

"Damn, you don't like me now?"

"That's not what I said. I'm saying…"

"How you live wit a nigga and don't like him. Damn am I that bad. C'mon man. You know I want to be with you." Guilt. It's shame's brother and they ride together. Right away my mind went back to that sad person I saw the night I left. Damn, damn, damn! I hate that I care.

"That's not what I meant. I do miss you too. I just don't want to live together. I just don't like living together. We just need to live separately. You have anger problems and…." My voice trailed off. I didn't want him to feel bad. Like he was unlovable or something. I thought, maybe I just won't talk about it. I mean, he knows he's fucked up and every time I say it his shoulders slump a little. He knows he bit me, slammed me into that stupid bike and choked me out. I don't like talking about it either. I gotta say something so he knows it's not that I don't like him, but that I don't like his outbursts. This shit is so crazy. Why do I care that he doesn't think it's him? He has trampled on my self esteem and kicked my ass.

"Marvin you can't hit me. I have never been hit before. I didn't even get hit as a kid. This is fucked up and I don't want to live with you right now." Lord please let him grab the 'right now' and run with it.

"A'ight. I know I was mad. You just be making me mad and shit. I don't even be tryna hurt you. You just be pissing me off, though. You could look up." I hadn't even realized I'd been talking into my lap the whole time. My brain was still in survival mode. Shame, guilt and confusion were driving my actions. I was not myself. I looked up, but held my gaze out the wind shield. I didn't really care to look over there. I knew what he thought. "So we good you just ain't wantin' to live together for a lil' while. That's cool." I knew better than to tell him the truth right then and context clues and body language meant nothing to him. Even if they did he'd ignore them to get the control of the situation he wanted. "You want me to drive you back to the house?"

"Hell no! Are you serious? My mom CANNOT know about this. Can't nobody know." My head was hung again. Dang, girl, hold your head up.

"Why? You told her? What did she say?"

"No I didn't tell her. She didn't like you anyway and I came home in the pouring rain with my bags packed. She knows shit ain't good over there or I wouldn't be here. My mama ain't stupid. She knows your whole family." As soon as I said it, I regretted it.

"My whole family? Fuck that supposed to mean?   What she said about my family?"

"I didn't say she said anything about them. I said she knows them. She didn't say anything. She just asked me if I was alright. She just doesn't need to know about me talking to you today. I'll walk back home."

"Home. You like throwing that shit in my face don't you? That's alright. Imma show you I can be nice and calm and shit. We'll see." Yeah, I'm so convinced. Not.

This muthafucker is crazy. God help me. "I'm going now. Ok?"

"Ok."

I got out of the car and put the hoodie back over my head. I closed the door and leaned my head in the window, "And you gotta stop calling my mom's house like that. Don't call there. I'll call you."

"Damn, I can't call you now? What…"

I interrupted, "Marvin, that is her house, you can't call there if she doesn't want you to. I will call you, alright?" He didn't answer. He hit the gas and the car sped off in reverse, tires screeching. Why don't I feel any better about this whole situation right now? I walked back to the house. I knew this was going to be a very hard situation to manage, but I was hopeful it would be easier managed living away from him than living with him. What am I managing? I'm still ♫ thinkin' of a master plan ♫ of how to get completely away from this dude, alive. When I got close to the house, I slowed my pace. I don't want to walk in winded, looking spent and breathing heavy. I had to keep my mom at arm's length too. That was a much easier task than dealing with Marvin.

Over the next few weeks I started going back to school and work, my back healed, the incessant telephone calls stopped, well, slowed significantly and I was able to talk to him from work, sneak and see him about once or twice a week and keep my mom calm. Whew! I was tired as hell. It was definitely a juggling act. I did feel like I was making progress with crazy. I was able to go out with my friends without him knowing and I was feeling like myself again. Gaining some of my confidence back. I decided to try to wean Marvin off the weekly visits so that I could get my _whole_ life back.

During one week I skipped a visit. I substituted a couple phone conversations and he didn't fuss about it too much. At this time I was working the 3pm to 11pm shift and I wanted to go out with my friends after work. I made sure I talked to him several times during my shift that day. I had also been talking to my best friend who was home from school visiting. There was something going on at a downtown club and we were definitely trying to be in the building that night. She was gonna pick me up, then we'd swing by my mom's house so I could change and it was going D.O.W.N.

Finally, some freedom. Some normalcy. I was amped to go. 11 o'clock couldn't come fast enough. At 11 on the dot she pulled up to the lobby doors and I darted out from the back office and jumped in the car. "What's up girl?"

"Nothing. Ready to get my pitcher!"

"Hell yeah!!!" We are going to have a ball. It was on and poppin! I got to the house, showered, changed, brushed my teeth and was back out in the car in 30 minutes. We drove to the downtown club, but parking was insane. We had to park in the parking lot across the street. There were a few cars in the lot, but I don't think the club goers had figured out they could park there after dark for free. We jumped out and made our way across the busy street toward the neon lights and winding line of people waiting to get their club on. This was back in the day of wearing sneakers to the club. Sneakers allowed for dancing, drinking without stumbling and running, if necessary. Sneakers also made waiting in that long ass line a lot more tolerable than it would have been in heels. We got inside and my girl got her pitcher. We start slowly moving around the club and we run into a high school classmate.

"What's up y'all?" He was screaming. The music was so loud I could feel it thumping inside my chest. "What y'all drinking on? That's sex on the beach?" He yelled with a hearty laugh.

"Hell yeah!" my girl screamed back.

"Damn girl! You got a pitcher?" He was cracking up by now.

"I need this to get me right!"

"Ok. I hear you. I hope I don't have to carry you outta here tonight!" Still yelling. He was joking but offering a friendly warning at the same time. He was cool as a fan and we all went way back. Back to like, kindergarten.

"Nah. I'm straight. I'm a soldier!" We all exploded with laughter.

"Who you in here with tonight? I know you ain't come out by yourself." She was asking him because there was likely to be an entourage of his friends that we knew too.

"Yeah, you know I ain't in here dolo. Mike, Kevin, Craig – they all in here somewhere. Probably harassing somebody's daughter. You know how that goes."

"Yeah I know. We'll see them. We just making our rounds." He nodded as he walked away waving a quick bye. We both waved back and kept walking around the perimeter of the dance floor. We were just basically trying to see who was there. What everyone was wearing and looking for a good spot. A good spot in the club meant a spot where we could lean on the wall, but still see the dance floor in case 'our song' came on. A spot where we could drink without 10 people bumping into us every few seconds. I sipped. She took it to the head. That's my girl.

The music was good, the drinks were right and all our friends were out tonight. We were having fun. Apparently everyone else was home from college visiting too. We saw so many people from high school that night. It was a crazy good time. And as crazy good times go in the club - inevitably this happens: You're standing slightly bobbing to the beat, sipping on a drink when the song changes and …. "Awwww shit! Hold my purse (drink, keys, wallet, I.D. – fill in the blank). That's my **SONG**!" I think this phrase is going to be on my girl's tombstone because I've heard her scream that more than anyone else I know.

As she beat a path to the dance floor, I sat her pitcher on the nearby table. It was mostly ice by then anyway and she had had enough. Just as she disappeared from my line of vision, someone called out my name. I turned to see a group of guy friends from school standing across the way. They were with our friend we had seen earlier.

"Hey! What's up!" I called back as I walked toward them. We greeted each other with hugs and laughs and a couple of them scooped me off my feet as they hugged me hello. We all stood around chatting and catching up as best we could in a loud, crowded club that was booming and thumping with bass-heavy music. They were all clowns and had me laughing the whole time we talked.

At one point one of the guys said, "Girl you know you're the only female over here talking to all us guys. You need to move before you cock block us all. These females ain't gonna believe we are all just friends with you." He had a point. "These dudes won't believe me when I tell them you're just my friends either. Y'all need to step away from ME!" We all laughed again and then dispersed after we hugged our goodbyes and well wishes. I walked around looking for my girl, slightly distracted by the music and somewhat by the drink too. There were lots of huge columns around the perimeter of the dance floor and near each entryway. I was trying to find her without going into that hot sweaty crowd. I'm short and I had on sneakers so I would find an opening and tippy toe to see as well as I could, then I'd move around until I saw the next opening and try to peek in again. I realized this technique was pretty much useless so I stopped and turned on my heels to head back to the spot we were standing when she went out to the dance floor.

As soon as I turned I bumped into someone. I looked up and almost shit my pants. It was Marvin. Holy Shit! Immediately and without hesitation I looked down at my feet. I didn't want my eyes to meet his. Fear surged through my body and I felt like my insides were on fire and viciously shaking. He leaned up against the column and crossed his feet so that I couldn't pass him without walking around him in an obvious way.

"What you doing out?" He said it in a low voice, but I heard it over the music and he knew I heard him. My lungs felt tight and I realized I wasn't breathing. I sucked in a long line of air and held it in. I was still looking down at the ground. All I saw were his shoes and his folded elbows. I didn't dare look up any higher.

"Fuck you doing in here? I know you heard me." His voice was more stern now. He was waiting for an answer. He had figured out that I had been plotting to get away from him all this week. And he knew why I'd talked to him so much today. Fuck! This was not the way I planned on this night going. He just blew any good time I was having. Buzz kill.

I was struggling to get my mind back to where I needed it to be to manage him in this environment. I had to keep him calm enough to not cause a scene in here. No one knew what I'd been living through and I didn't want them to find out by witnessing him flip out on me in a crowded club. I didn't want them to find out at all, but especially not like this. And especially not in front of this many other people. Childhood friends that never needed to know about any of this were here tonight. Damn! Think quick, think quick! "I came with my friend. She wanted to come and she didn't want to come by herself so I came with her. I

59

might have to drive her home cause she's been drinking tonight. That's all it was. No big deal."

"Why you ain't tell me then? Since it's no big deal you shoulda told me. Why you ain't tell me then?" He was squeezing his fingers on his forearms tighter and tighter. He was getting angry. I could see it. I could hear it in his voice. His voice was getting louder and he was grinding his teeth between each phrase. This isn't working.

"I didn't talk to you. She picked me up from work and we just came here. It wasn't a big plan or anything. Just spur of the moment."

"Did you call me from your house? Huh? You changed your clothes so I know you went home. You ain't call me from your house. Why not?"

I opened my mouth to answer and I felt a hand on my shoulder. "What's up girl? This dude trying to take you home or something?" It was one of my classmates. I was grateful and regretful because I knew he'd just saved me, but I also knew this would rear its ugly head again at a later date with Marvin. Letting go was not something he knew how to do. I turned and managed a smile. "You're silly. I already know him. But we did say this might happen, right?" He nodded. He turned to Marvin and offered his hand.

"What's up bruh? "

"Yeah." Marvin replied in a really shitty tone. He also avoided eye contact. Such a weirdo.

"Damn man. I'm just trying to be respectful and speak to you.   It's   like   that?"
"Nah, man. It's cool." Marvin extended his hand, but turned his head as he and my class mate shook hands. My friend looks at me and frowns as if to ask *what is wrong with this guy.* I nod my acknowledgment and shrug my shoulders. I truly do not know what is wrong with him.

"I'll see you later on, a'ight?" He looks me dead in the eyes when he says this and his message to me is loud and clear. 'I'll get you later.'

"Ok Marvin." I'm just glad this isn't going down tonight. Thank God for high school homeboys.

As soon as Marvin is out of sight he asks me, "What's up with that dude, man? He weird as fuck. That's your man or something? Why is he acting like that?" His face was still in a frown.

"We used to talk, but he's not my man anymore. You know how that goes."

"I guess. Let's go dance girl!" He scooped me up and threw me across his shoulder and ran to the dance floor. I'm screaming the whole way. Kicking and laughing. When he put me down I heard my girlfriend "HEEEEEEYYYY! This my shit! Where is my pitcher heffa?" I shrug and we start dancing. In minutes my world had returned to normal. I was glad. We danced through a couple more songs before the sex on the beach started tapping on my bladder. "I'll be right back! I gotta pee!" I screamed to her. She was sweating like crazy by then and I could tell she was not about to leave the dance floor.

I walked to the bathroom alone. It was disgusting as are most bathrooms inside the club. I washed my hands and walked out glad that I had on sneakers and just lip gloss. I would not want to be bothered with heels and liquid foundation in a bathroom like this. I felt his grip on my wrist and he snatched me around the corner. "Let's go outside and talk." He was basically dragging me. Damn! Had I been smarter, I would've known not to go anywhere in the club alone after my encounter with him earlier. But, I was still very naïve to the ways of an abuser.

When we got outside the club entrance one of the bouncers saw his grip on my arm and gave him a look. Marvin let go of my wrist and stepped behind me. He bent down and put his lips right at my ear "Walk to the car. Don't stop." I obeyed and walked straight ahead. "The car is right there across the street. In that parking lot." I looked up and I saw his car about 2 spaces down from my girlfriend's car. I felt trapped and more and more in danger the further I got from the neon lights of the club entrance. The music faded into the background. We got to the car and he unlocked the passenger door and gave me a slight push inside. I fell into the seat and he quickly locked the door from outside and jogged around to the driver's side and hopped in and locked his door as well. I turned my head and just stared out the passenger side window. He had me now. I was trapped. I didn't know half of what I needed to know and I didn't know nearly as much as I would learn before this entire ordeal of him in my life ended, but I knew that I was so exhausted from too many moments like this. He really needed help and I just wanted to lie down and sleep anytime I even thought of dealing with him. It was exhausting. He started in right away yelling and ranting and screaming. He was gripping the steering wheel and I had tuned him out before he got started. I just couldn't. I felt like I had almost had my real life back and he just wouldn't let me enjoy it. I was pissed and tired, a little tipsy and he was definitely killing my buzz.

I just wanted him to shut up and leave me alone. The noise he was making sharpened into identifiable words… "and who is that muthafucka trying to come in a keep you from talking to me? You know him? You fucking him? I ain't never heard you talk about him before! Who the fuck is he? And why you running around the club hugging and smiling up in all them fucking dudes faces? All them wanna fuck you! I know they do and there you are up in their faces laughing and shit like you so stupid you don't know they trying to fuck! You're so fucking stupid with that shit! You ain't giving me no pussy so I know you probably fucking one of them muthafuckas! Which one you fucking? Huh?"

I didn't even turn my head. I was just waiting for it to be over. Whatever was going to happen was going to happen. I had no more fight in me. I was done mind wrestling with him. I would just wait it out and try to stay alive. He was screaming as loud as he could when suddenly there was silence. Dead silence. It was completely quiet. Then slowly the ringing started and it got louder and louder and louder. He had slapped me. I'm sure he intended to hit me in the face, but instead he struck me directly on my ear. His hand had cupped my ear and everything had gone quiet for a few seconds. I still didn't react. I didn't even move. I just sat there. This infuriated him. He went ballistic! He started to beat his hands against the steering wheel. He was screaming and beating his hands against the dash and the steering wheel. I still held my gaze out the window. I didn't want to be a part of his temper tantrum. This was really adolescent. He was incapable of controlling himself. I turned to look at him because this was unbelievable.

BAM! My face met his clenched fist halfway into his swing. He landed a hard punch square on my cheekbone. My head ricocheted off his fist and slammed up against the car window. To this day I am still so shocked that the glass of that car window did not shatter into a million little pieces. I instantly burst into tears. It hurt so much. I had never felt pain like that. I had never been hit so hard in my life. My head throbbed right away. My sinuses burned and the pressure behind my eyes was unbearable. The tears hurt. When I clenched my eyes shut the pain made me scream out loud. It hurt like hell. I fumbled for the door handle, but it was still locked. I could see the condensation on the window every time I exhaled.

I couldn't move my head. It felt like it was stuck to the window. I tried to lift it, but he had his hand on the back of my head and he was slamming my head against the window as he gripped tighter on the fistful of my hair he had knotted into his fist. Each time my face hit the window he would press my head and hold it before he pulled back on my hair and slammed my head against the window for the next blow. When I reached to grab the lock on the door I felt his other hand on top of mine trying to press the lock back down, but it was too late. I had managed to unlock the door. I felt a patch of my hair rip from the back of my head as I fell out of the car onto the concrete. I was on my knees so I just started crawling as fast as I could toward the back of the car. Thinking back that was crazy. He could have run me over had he started the car and put it in reverse which he could easily have done since he was still in the driver's seat when I fell out onto the ground. When I got to the rear of the car I pulled myself up and rested on the trunk of the car. I was panting and holding my head. It still hurt so much. I felt the motor of the car begin to vibrate so I stepped away from the back tire. Everything was blurry.

I saw a police cruiser slowly driving up one of the aisles of the parking lot. I started feverishly waving my hands in the air and screaming, "Help! Help! Please help me!" Marvin had also eyed him which was why he'd started the car. He was going to run. I didn't care. I was alive. I started to run away from Marvin's car and toward the police car. The cruiser came to a slow stop and I leaned against the hood of the officer's car exhausted, "Please officer…help me." I saw the flashing lights begin to dance atop his car and I felt so relieved. Dear God, finally, some help. I felt the car sway slightly as the officer shifted it into park. I laid my head on the hood of the cruiser.

I heard the wheels of Marvin's car screech as he bolted from the parking lot. The officer opened the car door and slammed it shut. I could hear his footsteps approaching me and I exhaled what felt like all the air in my body.

Chapter 5

The police officer came around to where I was stretched out on the hood of his car. He leaned up against the passenger side door and folded his arms in front of him. "Ma'am what's the problem?" He didn't sound like I thought he'd sound. I still couldn't move. The back of my head was throbbing. My face was throbbing and I could have sworn my jaw was broken. My hands were scraped from crawling on the concrete and my knees were sore from when I'd fallen out of the car. I still did not move. I was sprawled out on the hood of the poe poe's car panting like a sick dog. Damn I'm glad I wore sneakers tonight. I felt the car sway slightly again. The officer had taken his weight off the car. He walked around me. As he rounded the front of the car he said, "Ma'am you need to get up. Get off the vehicle." Huh? Is this dude yelling at me? I heard the car door slam as he got back into his car. I was stumbling around the front of the car and hitting the hood of the car with my hand. He was cranking the car up! No! No! No! No! He cannot leave me out here like this. I need him to chase that fool down and arrest his ass! No! No! Wait.

"Officer! No! Wait! Wait a minute! I need you to go arrest him. He just punched me and smashed my head against the window and pulled my hair and drug me outta the club!" I probably sounded like a rambling idiot. I could hardly get the words out fast enough. "He's in a box Chevy. Four door. It's tan. I think he's on probation too!" Yeah I just punked all the way out. Broke all the 'codes' and told everything. I didn't give a damn. I was tired of being pounded on. Enough of this craziness. In all of that confusion the officer just sat there. He didn't rush off behind him or anything. He didn't even put his car into drive. He just sat there. By this time I was at the driver side window of the patrol car. The cop was sitting there behind the wheel. He had his head cocked to the side and he rolled his eyes. What the fuck! Aye, you need to be on some Dukes of Hazard type shit right now. Peel out motherfucker! Go get his ass! He just sat there! I was jumping up and down at this point. "I'm for real! Look at my face! He did this to me and he's right there! He just drove off! He's right there! You could still catch up to him!" I broke down into tears. I mean sniffling, stuttering, slobbering tears.

The ~~asshole~~ cop looks at me and says, and I quote, "Let me tell you how these things go, ok? I waste a whole lotta my time and go after this guy. I get your statement, write a report and turn all this crap in." What is really going on here? I can't with this damn poe leece man, MAN! What is he saying right now? He continues, "And then the court date comes and goes and you never show up. You forgive him and you two get back together and I've wasted a whole lotta my time. All for nothing. I've seen it a thousand times before."

If you could've seen this dude's face! Really though. "Are you really gonna follow thru with this? Or are you just gonna be back with this same guy next week who just beat you up tonight? You tell me." By this time, Messy is so far gone I know the cop couldn't catch him now anyway. I looked at the empty parking lot. I looked down at my scraped up hands. I touched the back of my head. My damn face is still throbbing. My entire face is throbbing. The side that he slammed up against the car window and the side he slammed his fist against. I stood there and began to brew. I was getting pissed! This is some bullshit! I had not done anything wrong and I felt like I was being punished. Marvin was punishing me for simply greeting my friends during a fun night out at the club and now this disrespectful ass cop was completely violating me again and putting me in harm's way because he 'thought' I'd end up back with my abuser. I was having an Incredible Hulk moment. The little green guy was growing inside me. The only people there at the time were me and the police officer. He may not have come to my rescue, chased the bad guy or written a report, but dammit he's gonna hear me out tonight.

"You know what? Fuck you! Yeah, fuck you. Your car says you're here to protect and serve and tonight you failed at both. You didn't do either. You came up on a scene and you saw me, a victim, standing here needing assistance. Whether or not you believe I will run back to him or not, you are supposed to do your damn job. Your job is to assist the victim, get the bad guy and write the fucking report, you dick!. You're an asshole. I just might have been the one who would have shown up for the court date. Or I might be the one who goes back because you didn't do your job tonight and ends up dead. Your job is not to judge me you asshole! Fuck off!" And I walked off - Like a boss!

He sat there for a moment. A short time later I heard him slowly drive away. I don't know what he thought about what I said to him or what happened that night, but I do know he didn't expect what came out of my mouth to come out of my mouth that night.

I'm out here in the dark by myself walking around this parking lot with a patch of hair missing and bruised face. I can't let my girlfriend see me like this, but I have no ride home. Plus she's my ace and she won't just leave without me or leave without knowing I'm ok. I need to put a note on her car and find a way to get home so I can clean myself up. Clean myself up, AGAIN! I walked back across the street and asked the guy at the door if I could get a piece of paper and use his pen to write a quick note to my friend in the club. He gave me a pen and a tiny piece of paper. I could feel his eyes on me while I wrote. When I finished I handed him the pen back. I had no idea how I looked. He looked at me with a really sad face. "You alright baby girl?" He slid the pen back into his pocket, but he didn't take his eyes off me.

"Yeah, I'm good. Thanks for the pen and paper." I hated being looked at like that, ya know? Like I'm someone to be pitied or something. Like someone should feel sorry for me. Or like, damn that's a shame she gets treated like that. For all dude knew I could've been in a scuffle with another female. That's not the look I got from him though. And for all *I* know, he could've seen the whole thing take place. I was embarrassed. That was one of the times I specifically remember being embarrassed about what was going on in my life with Marvin. I never wanted anyone to know what was going on because I figured I would feel ashamed or embarrassed, but the way the doorman looked at me confirmed what I'd thought. This shit is embarrassing as hell.

With my head hung I walked back across the street to the dark parking lot. I was so naïve I still didn't think to be afraid. I mean, he could easily have come back had he wanted to. I walked up to my girlfriend's car and slid the lie under the windshield wiper. That was my girl, but I couldn't bear to let her know about this wild shit that was now my reality. I started walking. I had no idea where I was going. Somewhere into the night. I knew I had to find the answer or at least find a way to make it to tomorrow so I could deal with the aftermath.

The night wind from the ocean had made its way over the bridge. It was cool against my skin. My face and the back of my head were burning though. Had I not just got me ass kicked it would've been a nice enjoyable walk in the cool night air. As I'm walking I'm thinking. Always thinking. That was probably one of the things that kept me moving forward. I had taken a lot of blows. To my body, to my confidence and to my mind, but I never stopped thinking and moving forward in my head. I always had thoughts of how I could get away from him. Or thoughts of my life once I did get away from him. There were definitely times when I didn't know how it would happen. And there were also times when I thought I might not ever be able to get away from him or get away from him alive, but I always thought about it or fantasized about it. Life after Messy Marvin.

During that walk I came up with a plan to hide what had happened from my mom. I had braids in my hair at the time. When he pulled that plug out of my hair he left a patch in the back. I would pretend that I was just ready to take my braids down so that my mom wouldn't be too suspicious. Now about my face...I didn't know how bad it looked. I just knew how bad it felt. When I got in the house I went straight to the bathroom and flipped on the light. DAYUM! My hair looked like a mango seed. It was sticking straight up in the back and it was just tore up from the floor up. It was all stringy and uneven and ratty looking. I turned a little to the side so I could see how big the patch was. I was too afraid to get the hand held mirror and really get a full view of it. Lord knows what I would see back there. Probably blood. It looked a hot shitty mess from the side. I could see that it wasn't as big a plug as I thought. I could pull my hair up into a ponytail or a bun and get away with it. At least until my scalp wasn't so sore.

Surprisingly my face didn't look bad. It hurt like a mofo, but it didn't look as bad as it felt during or after the Tasmanian devil attack. It looked like I had been in the sun too long. Who knows what it will look like by the time I wake up tomorrow, well today, it was already like 3 in the morning.

I woke up to hearty laughter. It was a voice I recognized. It was my brother. I didn't realize he was in town. He always laughed so loud. A Santa Clause kind of laugh. I felt better. I felt safe and protected. I didn't realize how unprotected I had felt before. I guess having Taz jump on you and sling you around a parking lot could make you feel unprotected, though. I got up and slid into the bathroom to see what my face looked like before I went out front. And I had to put my hair up into that bun.

72

My scalp was still throbbing. Hallelujah! I didn't bruise. This is how sick the shit gets. I'm in the bathroom doing a happy dance because my face didn't bruise from being beat. So sad. *sigh* I went into the living room and there was my brother, sitting talking with my mom. He greeted me as usual with his big hearty laugh. About 2 minutes in I knew my mom had talked to him because he asked me if I wanted to take a ride to the store with him. That was clearly a sign of him trying to get me by himself so he could talk to me. I knew this trick. We got in the car and headed out of the driveway. Then out of my neighborhood. We ended up in the parking lot of McDonald's eating fries and vanilla ice cream.

"So baby sis, what's going on?"

"Nothing much." He gave me a face. "What? Why you looking at me like that? Ain't nothing going on."

"That ain't what mom said. Who is this dude?"

Now, let me pause for the cause here and give you a bit of background so you understand why this lie that's about to come out of my mouth, comes outta my mouth. I have a lot of brothers and cousins and they are all pretty much crazy when it comes to the women in the family. All of them will get in your ass; several of them will fuck you up at the drop of a dime; and some of them will put your face in the dirt just for GP (general purposes). Let me also explain that there are also lots of women in my family. Mostly pretty petite women. Women who may be likely to date or be desired by many men.

This means, those women are also more likely to run into some assholes. Just speaking mathematically it's probably gonna happen that a nigga will need his ass put in a sling about fucking with a female in the family I'm from. It's something I grew up knowing. I heard stories all my life about this type behavior from the older men in my family. I had uncles who had fought dudes in the streets for mistreating my aunts and such. There's a story about one of my brothers finding out that a cousin of mine had been slapped by a guy she was seeing. My brother and a cousin went looking for the guy. When they found him my cousin held him still while my brother proceeded to beat him down. At some point during this ass whuppin the guy broke free from my cousin's grip. So what do these two do? Chase dude down and drag him back to where they were originally fighting. Apparently he didn't make it too far.

My brother says he was tired from chasing the guy, but now he was mad at my cousin for letting the dude squirm out of his grip so he wanted to hold the guy down and continue delivering blows. So he wraps his fist in the guy's t-shirt and turns, and turns, and turns until the shirt is so tight the guy can't move but a few inches at a time. But he doesn't hit him. He just sits there. He says he was tired and he needed to catch his breath before he started in on round 2 of the ass-kick mission. So he and my cousin are there breathing hard and trying to catch their breath while the guy is kicking and squirming trying to free himself. Once they'd rested up they proceeded to beat this snot out of this guy some more.

That's just one story of many so I knew this conversation was real. So in the interest of Marvin's life, health and physical safety, I lied. Why? Why wouldn't I want them to pound him? Shouldn't I want him beat senseless by grown men who could easily overpower him and make him sorry for every single time he had laid a hand on me or every time he'd stomped on my spirit? It's a part of the mind-fuck that happens to you when you are in an abusive relationship. It's very real, but it's very irrational. Unless you've been there, it's difficult to understand it. The best way I can describe it is like this: If you get an F on a test, you know that's bad. If you then take another test and you get a D, as bad as a D is, you can feel some happiness about having received a grade of D instead of F. That happy dance I did in the bathroom because my face wasn't bruised, yeah that was my D. This happens in a very subtle way and I don't know of any woman who has been abused who says she knew what was going on psychologically while it was happening.

So during those times when you are not in the midst of the storm, you tend to minimize the severity of it all. I also had developed a sense of care and concern for him. It was because I knew how screwed up he was. I had seen the sad, insecure and vulnerable person that lived inside him and caused him to respond to the world the way he did. That quality in my personality is something I feel abusers pick up on extremely quickly. It's like a pimp and a hoe. They know in minutes whether or not you possess the personality traits that would allow them that get into your psyche. So as completely irrational as it sounds to say it, it is a reality of lots of abusive relationships women find themselves in. That is why they go back time and time again and place themselves in harm's way. Sad, but true. Now, back to the lie…

"He's not a bad guy. He really isn't . She just knows his family and they got some wild ones so I think she is just concerned. Hell if somebody looked at us they may think I was a bad choice too. Ya know?" He gave me another look. He wasn't really buying it, but I was selling hard. This had to fly. I didn't want them to kill him. I really didn't want him dead. I didn't even really want him hurt. I just wanted away from him. I just wanted to be safe. And more so, I didn't want anyone to know what I had let happen to me. "What? I'm just saying. Y'all are crazy and I'm related to y'all so if people didn't know they may think I was crazy too."

"Are you alright, though?"

"Yeah, I'm good. I'm good." I tried to sound as upbeat and perky as I could while my scalp throbbed and my face burned.

"Has he hit you yet?" He leaned back in his chair.

"Damn man. What you mean yet? No he has never hit me. I told you I'm good. I don't want to keep talking about this. You ready?" Lord please let him let this go.

"Nah, I wanna finish my fries. Then we can go." He was looking straight through me. Brewing. I knew he knew I was lying. I wondered what all my mother had told him and how much she actually knew. You know moms have a way about them. They always seem to find out the real, especially when you're trying to hide it from them while living in their house. I just looked straight ahead and tried to avoid his gaze. I felt his eyes on me though. He saw everything I wished wasn't there. The shame, the embarrassment, the guilt and the anguish. I knew he saw it and even though I was as still as the night I was screaming out for help inside. Hoping that he heard beyond my silent lies.

We drove in silence. No words from either of us. I don't know who was more uncomfortable. Me, hoping he'd floor it so we could get home and I could get the hell outta this car, or my brother who drove slower than necessary while trying to hold in his rage. We pulled onto our street and he broke the silence. "When are you moving out of mom's house?"

"I've been looking around. Probably the next couple months or so."

"I'll be here for a while. You don't need to be alone so I'm gonna move in with you."

"How you know I want you living with me?" He knew I was joking and we both laughed a bit. It eased the tension.

"Whatever. You better be cooking while I'm there too. Spoiled ass." He smiled at me. I felt such a sense of relief. It was the first time since I'd found myself trapped that I could see light at the end of the tunnel. I was happy. When we pulled up to the house he parked the car and looked over at me. "You *did* break up with him, right?"

"Yeah, I did." Funny, but we hadn't spoken a word about the status of the relationship. Yeah, he definitely knew I had been lying.

We went inside the house and he gave my mom the nod. The nod that said, yeah I got this. I'm handling the situation. She acknowledged his nod and then told me that my girl friend had called while we were gone. I figured they had some conspiring to do so I took the phone and went into the bedroom to return the call. I started to think on the way into the bedroom that maybe my mom had told my girlfriend what she suspected was going on between me and Messy. Damn, I hope not. My friend was too outspoken for me to manage her on top of everything else that was going on at the moment.

"Hello."

"Hey. You called me?"

"Damn girl. Where you disappeared to last night? Was the shit good?" We had been friends since life began. Since her life began, anyway, I'm the oldest. We had known each other literally our entire lives. We were past the point where every torrid detail was necessary. That was the case when we were much younger maybe, but now all we needed was an affirmation about whether or not *it* had been good.

"Hell yeah. Just a lil something I had to go take care of."

"Who? Marvin lil thin ass?" We laughed. She really didn't know. I breathed a sigh of relief that she mistook as an expression of how 'good' it had been last night. Last night was anything but good.

"Damn, like that? Ok then. I hear you. What you doing now?"

"Nuttin, just got back from Mickey D's."

"Ok. Want me to come pick you up so we can ride through the park?"

"Yeah, lets go." Oh shit. What if he's there?

Chapter 6

I found an apartment I liked a lot. It was a brand new complex. The developer was staying at the hotel where I had been working and he gave me the heads up. It was nice and cozy. I choose a unit in the back of the complex that was nestled in a nice little corner. It seemed safe and out of the way of mainstream traffic. It was spacious and I was happy with it. Although the deal had been for my brother to move in, he didn't exactly live there. He was there a lot and sometimes he'd spend the night, but he still didn't truly live there.

My new place was about a 20 minute walk from where he lived. I knew if I called he could be there fast. The apartment smelled like a new building when I moved in. The walls were stark white and the counter tops still had little specs of dust on them from construction. There was a small tiled entry way that led into the living area. To the right was a huge bay style window. I wasn't too fond of that, but it would do. It felt like people could look in at me and I don't like that kind of layout to this day. The window was almost the length of the wall and I decided to put a dining set there and cover the window with dark window dressings. If you stood at the front door and turned your head left you'd be looking into the guest bedroom.

Just past the entryway and on the left side of the apartment was the kitchen. It was standard. Super white with a basic refrigerator, stove and small dishwasher. The cabinets were a stone grayish color with tiny little flecks of pink scattered in. It was an odd combination and it made the kitchen feel cold when you took in the cabinets against the blinding white walls. Everything was brand new which helped. I couldn't imagine how it would look with spots or dirt or just the stains that come with everyday wear and tear on that white, gray and pink canvas.

Wrapped around to the left side of the kitchen was the guest bedroom. If you walked through the kitchen into that bedroom you would eventually end up back at the front entryway. It just looked like 4 walls. And that's all it was. No windows, no fancy architecture, just a room. The carpet in the bedroom was a little more plush than the run of the mill thin layer that covered the living area. Straight ahead from the entry way was the master bedroom. The room was pretty big. It had a nice layout. There was a small window to the right of the door and to the left was a small closet which sat just at the entrance to the bathroom. To the right of the entrance to the bathroom was a medium sized walk in closet. There were flakes of white dust on the carpet inside the main closet and you could still see markings and numbers that had been penciled in by the construction workers when they were affixing the shelves to the walls. It smelled like fresh paint in there.

I stepped into the bathroom and looked in the mirror. The mirror was long and rectangular with no border. It hung above the sink and spread across the entire wall from right to left. Next to the sink was a porcelain toilet. Brand new and unused. It's a funny thought to look at a commode and think – wow no shit or piss has touched this yet. Just a thought I had. Behind the sink was a small tub. Above it was a thin metal rod to hang a shower curtain. I tapped the tub with my big toe. It was hollow and as cheap as they come. It was nothing like the tub in my mom's house. That thing was built and installed back in the day and it was solid. Kick it if you want to. You would probably limp away with a sore foot. The floors of the bathroom and kitchen were covered with off white linoleum that had tan outlines of squares that formed a tile-like print. I turned back to the mirror and looked at myself. I hope this works out. I really do. I hope he just fades away into my past so I can get back to a normal existence. I folded my hands together into a knot and placed them under my chin. I closed my eyes and prayed a little prayer to God. "Please help me get out of this mess I'm in. I want to be ok and I want to get back to myself. Please God help me. Amen." When I opened my eyes I jumped and screamed a little scream. "Oh shit!" There was a face in the mirror beside mine.

"Girl calm down!" It was my stupid ass brother.

"Can your ass knock? You scared me half to death!"

"I don't know what that nigga did to you, but you need to calm down. You ready?"

"Get out! Give me 5 minutes." We were going to look at furniture for the apartment. I had nothing. I was starting from scratch so this would be a process. I slammed the bathroom door and splashed some water on my face. I opened the door and grabbed the roll of paper towels that was on the floor of the bedroom. I had to pee, but I didn't have any toilet paper or soap. Oh well. I took the roll into the bathroom and christened the virgin toilet. Welcome to the real world. I flushed, washed my hands and walked into the living room where my brother was propped up against the counter in the kitchen. "I'm ready."

I had an idea of what I wanted. I liked white. I always have. I still do. I picked out a sofa, loveseat and two end tables. Signed on the dotted line and scheduled a delivery date. It was simple. I had been working and saving money and I knew what I wanted and how much I could spend. When we got back into the car, my brother asked me what I planned to do about getting my own car. I had been thinking about this too. I needed a car. I had been working at the hotel for about a year at this point, but it wasn't enough. A guest had told me about some openings at the nearby branch of the post office and I had already gone in and applied. If they called and I got hired, I had no idea how I'd get back and forth to 2 jobs. ♫ thinking of a master plan ♫ I knew the job at the post office was seasonal, but I also knew that if I could work both jobs for a few months I would have enough to buy a car. The new apartment wasn't expensive and this second job would basically be for the sole purpose of purchasing a vehicle. I made enough to handle the apartment and a car. I just needed the money for a down payment.

"I've been thinking." I gave him a side eyed glance.

"And?"

"So how about if you keep chauffeuring me around like you've been doing for a little bit longer. I have a plan in place. I applied at the post office for a seasonal position. If I work that for a few months I can save enough to put down on a car. I just need some time. Can you keep driving Miss Daisy?"

"Do you have the job yet?"

"No, but I know I'm gonna get it. Not worried about that. I'm more worried about how I'm gonna get to and from."

"So you just sure, huh? You are cocky as hell. You know that?"
"I ain't cocky. I just know I can get a job. How hard can it be to impress them in an interview? *Yes sir I can sort envelopes and put them in a slot.* C'mon man. I got this."

"A'ight if you think so, then whatever. How you plan on working 2 jobs?"

"I work 3 to 11 now so I'll do the overnight shift at the post office. They have an 11pm to 7am shift. It's right around the corner from the hotel. I could walk if I have to…" He cut me off.

"Nah, I'll drive you. You damn sure don't need to be walking at 11 at night. You're gonna be late every day. You can't end a shift and start one at the same time."

"Man, I got this. You just chauffeur and let me fuck this cow. I know what I'm doing."

"Ok."

"You gon' do it?"

"Yeah. How long do you think you need before you can buy a car?"

"Probably 2 – 3 months."

"Ok. That's cool."

Things were looking good. I was gonna be one tired lil mama, but you do what you gotta do. I wanted to get back to school and get things back on track. I had bigger plans for myself than this deadbeat life I had going on at the moment. The shit sucked to be honest with you, but you have to endure sometimes to get to the other side.

The furniture came and it livened up the place a lot. I got the job at the post office and my brother was still playing body guard/chauffeur. Things were looking up in a lot of ways, but there were things I noticed about myself that were different than before. I was always nervous. Constantly expecting something to happen. If my brother was watching TV and he laughed I would jump out of my skin. Many times I would wake up in the middle of the night panicked or having some crazy dream. The dreams of him chasing me were the worst. In the dream I would be running as fast as I could run, but my body would be moving in slow motion. I would be screaming, but no sound would come out and although there were people all around me in the dream, they couldn't hear me screaming.

I never actually saw him in these dreams. I could just feel his presence. He would be getting closer and closer and I knew he was close to me but I couldn't see exactly where he was and I couldn't run any faster or scream any louder. Scary. I knew my family had an idea that things had gone on between us, but nobody knew how bad it really was for me while I lived with him. I didn't talk about it. I felt like they wouldn't understand or that they'd blame me for staying as long as I had or for getting involved with him in the first place.

When you're not equipped to manage an abusive relationship you find yourself bombarded with emotions and feelings that are beyond the scope of what you know to be normal. When there are no friends or family members for you to confide in or get advice from, you feel very alone. And you feel responsible for being in that type of situation. For me, I lied and hid as much of it as I could because I was ashamed and embarrassed and I felt like I should have known better or I should have been able to see it coming and avoid it. I didn't know how I ended up being stuck in a situation that had become so violent and so dangerous. I was a good girl and I shouldn't have been in that.

A lot of self loathing can come from the mental games you play with yourself when your self esteem has been trampled on. The loneliness leads you back to the abuser sometimes too. You feel like he's the only other person that understands. It's almost like you're in it together. Many times I found myself hoping beyond hope that I could somehow go back and fix him so that we could have a normal relationship. If that could have happened it would have all made sense. I could have held my head up high and said to everyone – "See we made it. I'm being treated well." Then the lies I'd told and the covering up I had done wouldn't have been in vain. That is part of the reason it is so hard to get out and get out safely. Your mind is fucked up. It wasn't my fault and I needed help to get out, but at the time I was so unaware of that.

There were sometimes when my brother would pick me up and drop me off and at other times he would let me drive his car. Things seemed to have calmed down. No instances of Messy in about 3 weeks or so. I think we were all still nervous but it seemed under control. More under control than it had been for me before. I think he had dialed my mom's number a time or two, but she knew how to handle that. And I hadn't spoken to him since before I moved so I knew he didn't know where I lived. I was scared as hell at times though. When I would think about that idiot in my mother's house crouched down and wedged between the toilet and the damn sink I would get nervous.

Crazy is a no-limit soldier. It'll do any damn thing. One of the nights when I had my brother's car I was rushing to get from the hotel to the post office and as I got into the car a strange sense came over me. When freaky shit like 'strange senses' happen, always, always, always pay attention to what you feel. It never lies. I tried to ignore it, but I couldn't shake the feeling. It felt like someone was in the car. Oh hell. I turned the car off and got out. I walked around the entire car looking up and down and underneath the car. I know, I know, like the dumb ass girl in the movie that ends up dead. I bent down slowly, but I chickened out so I backed up a few feet. Hell if something or someONE *was* **under** the car I didn't want to give them a clear shot at my face. I bent down again and peered under the car. There was nothing. I jumped the hell up because I could have sworn I heard a noise behind the car. Screw this! I jumped in the car and started the engine.

If something was behind the car it was about to get run the hell over. I threw it in reverse, hit the gas, then the brake and then threw it into drive and floored it out of the parking lot. As I was driving I kept looking in the rear view mirror, but I didn't see anything. You would think that was good, but I wanted to see whatever had spooked me so that I could ID it and then calm down. Not knowing was worse. I pulled up to the post office and got out of the car. I was headed toward the door when I remembered I left my badge in the back seat. Damn! I'm already running late. I turned back to get it and it hit me. I hadn't checked the back seat of the car at the hotel. I did not want to, but I had to look in the back seat and I had to hurry THEE hell up and get on with it so I could get to work. Damn! Damn! Dayum Gina! Now looking in the back seat would have been a little easier had my brother not copped a freakin' mini van! So I had to slide the 10 ft long door all the way back and then look *inside* while I'm *outside* in the pitch blackness of the night. Lord, hold my mule!

This shit is way scarier than Freddy Kruger and Jason because this is real life. I took a deep breath and just slid the door open as fast as I could. I'm waiting to scream. I'm waiting to scream. I'm waiting to scream. Whew! Nothing. Thank goodness. There was no one in the back seat waiting to stab me to death. I grabbed my badge and ran inside the building. All was well right? Not exactly. That feeling I had was real and it was dead on. Marvin had been out of sight, but he was not out of mind. He had been following me for weeks. He knew where I lived. He knew where I was working and he knew that my brother was watching my back.

He was lurking around corners and taking notes. He had been watching, plotting, planning and waiting. The loss of control had driven him to new heights of insanity. Your mind body and spirit will always tell you the truth. You just have to learn to listen to it. My grandmother always said listen to your mind. It's the truth. Every time I had felt that little tingle of fear and goose bumps rose up on my arms, he was watching me. I believe that now. He was watching all the while. Soon he would act and it would not be pretty.

Chapter 7

It had been about 2 months and even though I still had some uncertainty about Messy Marvin, I was starting to relax a lot more. I hadn't spoken to him or seen him since that night in the parking lot. Honestly, the silence kind of creeped me out, but time had passed and I felt a lot better. I was going to be working at the post office for another 4 to 5 weeks and things at the hotel were going well. My brother was around most of the time and I had finally saved enough money to buy a car of my own. I ended up rolling off the lot with a Nissan Maxima.

It was fly. At least I thought so. It was a cute little silver deal with a light tint on the windows. I was in business now. It felt really nice to be on my own, working, living in my own place and with my own transportation. After about a week or so, I started to go to work and back home by myself in my new car. For the first few days my brother would drive to the hotel at the end of my shift and either follow me to the post office or follow me home. I was more conscious of my surroundings than I had ever been before, but I was ok coming and going alone.

Since the incident in the parking lot and moving into my place I hadn't even entertained the thought of going out or dating or anything of the sort. I was focused at the time on getting away from Marvin and handling my situation. Now that things had calmed I felt like I could get back out into the world a little more. At least go out with my friends and have a good time and see what was out there. That was the thought, but I was honestly still a little nervous about running into him. The city wasn't but so big and it was bound to happen at some point. My hope was that enough time had passed to send him the message that I wanted out and that it was over. I didn't know how much time he needed to get that, but he hadn't been around (from what I knew at the time) and I had made no attempts to contact him so it should have been very clear. I was ready and my friends had been giving me a hard time anyway about being lame and never hanging out. I decided that the next time an opportunity presented itself I was going to take it.

That chance came about a week after I had that conversation with myself. See how you start to go crazy your damn self? Having conversations with myself was not good. My ace, called me and was crunk and ready to put down a couple pitchers of sex on the beach and scrub the ground. She called one Friday night.

"What you doing?"

"Nothing girl. What's up?"

"You working one of your 15 jobs tonight?"

"Nah girl. And I only have 2 jobs."

"Bet! Let's go to the club."

"A'ight. What you wearing?" Isn't this always the question that follows confirmation that you're going to the club? Women, we have to be on the same page with the wardrobe. I really don't think dudes do this to themselves.

"I don't know. Some jeans probably. I'm tryna scrub the ground and get my drank on!"

"Ok. Imma wear some jeans too then. What time you wanna get there?"

"Early. I need to get my money's worth and drinks are free before midnight."

"You are a damn drunk! We can get there at 11 then. You want me to come pick you up?"

"Yeah. And hoe you be drinking right along with me."

"Whatever! I'll call you when I'm on my way. Bye!"

"Bye!"

I got myself up and got dressed. I had on my tightest, most yeast infectiony-est, coochie cutting-est jeans, my favorite black fur cropped top and my most comfortable non-sneaker black shoes to match my top. My hair was done, my nails were done and I was ret ta go! I hopped in the car and zoomed to her house while blasting my best pre-club music. What's pre-club music? It's just basically music to get you hyped up before you get to the club so that you're in the right mood when you arrive. So I scooped my girl and we made our way to the club. We threw our purses in the trunk of the car and headed in. Line outside = Free. 2 pitchers of Sex On The Beach = $10 each. Scrubbing the ground and a helluva time with my ace = Priceless! We made our way to the dance floor and proceeded to ♫drop it like it's hot. drop it like it's hot ♫ The DJ was in full effect and even though the club was damn near empty that early, we were already having a good ole time. As the night wore on the club thickened up quite nicely. We meandered through the crowd, both on pitcher number 2. Eventually we made our way around the perimeter of the club. You always gotta make a few rounds just to see what else is going on besides the fun on the dance floor.

While we were making our rounds I saw him! Hot damn! I knew I was gonna see him up in here tonight. I had a feeling before I left the house that it would go down like this tonight. 'Damn. I've been drinking and shit.' I cursed myself. I need to really get myself together before he sees me. I'm so glad I saw him first. I yank my girl by the arm.

"Girl! Look who is up in this muthafucker tonight!" See squinted her eyes, looked out in the crowd, opened her eyes wide, squinted again.

"Damn you are blind as hell! He's right there! You can't see that?" She was really blind as hell. Picture Fred Sanford when puts his ~~goggles~~ glasses on. I grabbed her head with both my hands and turned it in the direction I had been pointing. "Right there!"

"Awwww shit! That's my song!" She turned and before I knew what to do she was gone like a flash headed straight to the dance floor. Pitcher in hand.

"Damn." I said it under my breath. This girl just left me over here by myself. Ain't that a bitch? Let me run to the bathroom to get myself together before he sees me. You ever go into the bathroom at the club and look in the mirror and realize you do not look as cute as you thought you did when you left home? LOL! I was having one of those moments. I looked in the mirror and I just saw a greasy face and red eyes. I grabbed a paper towel and wiped my face. This was long before the days of a beat face so there was no powdering of the nose just a wipe down with a dingy paper towel in the ladies room. Whew. Let's get back out here and get this over with. I came out of the bathroom and walked over to him. He was standing there leaning back with his elbow on the bar behind him. I figured if I walked up to him he'd be forced to say something to me.

"What's up?" He spoke softly and gave a small smile.

"Nothing much. What's up with you?" I was so nervous.

"You. That's what's up." Oh shit. What was I supposed to say to that? I am terrible at this. And I think I'm buzzed which is not helping right now. Where in the hell was my partner? She should be over here helping me with this dude.

"I'm saying. What you getting yourself into? What you doing out here tonight? This ain't even your style. I ain't never seen you in here before. Why you out here?" By now I'm shaking in my boots and my heart is pounding like crazy.

"Ummmm…"

"She's in here tryna holla at you. You know why she's in here. Why you tryna call her out?" Thank the Lord! She came through in the crunch. I don't know what I would've done had she not shown up when she did. She was not nervous of course because she wasn't checking for dude like I was. I had been trying to get close to this guy for a minute now.

"We'll talk to y'all later." She walks away and I quickly follow.

"Why you left?"

"Girl, we can talk to them later. Right now I'm trying to get my dance and drank on." Whatever. I guess I'd see him later. It wasn't like I hadn't already been waiting months. This guy was so intriguing to me. I'd been wanting to see what his deal was for the longest time. I had seen him out before, here or there, and every time I saw him he was dressed to a T, hair cut fresh to death, dark skinned like I like 'em and just had a smoothness about himself that was attractive. I had heard so much about him, but I wanted to know for myself. There was something about him that I really found attractive. The couple times I'd heard him talk he was so damn cool with it too. Everything about him turned me on. All of it.

She proceeded to get her dance and drank on until the lights in the club came on. Talk about sweating in the club, yo! My girl holds the record! To this day. For real! She wiped herself down, we put the pitchers on the counter and we headed out for a lil parking lot pimping. You have to hit the parking lot after the club. It's just the way it goes. This particular night we did our pimping in the parking lot of the local fast food restaurant. We had to hurry or we wouldn't get a good spot. I mean, the parking lot is only so big and err body went there so the spots went quickly. We made it there and I backed into a spot near the entrance. I rolled down all the windows and played my music on low. The parking lot was new. The white stripes that outlined the spaces were still bright white and the asphalt was pitch black beneath the stripes. I lined my car up perfectly in the spot and we sat there for a minute. Peeping out the prospects. My ace was checking for this dude David. The good thing about that was that David was tight with the dude I had been trying to push up on. We were hoping they'd both come through the parking lot that night. But while we sat and hoped, we saw some other good tasty treats floating through. Eye candy ain't never a bad thing. And soon enough we saw the real prize ride through.

"There they go!"

"Yep! Let's get out."

"Ok."

We checked our lip gloss and hair and got out real slow and calm. You can't be too hyped because you may come across desperate. Gotta keep ya cool and play it smooth. We walked to the front of the car and sat on the hood. There was a reason I had backed into the spot. Soon enough they walked by where we were - just as planned. Yeah, they were feeling us too. My girl and David walked a few steps away and talked about whatever it was they had going or were trying to get going. I, on the other hand, sat there on the hood of my car and talked to the man of the hour. This dude had me mesmerized for some reason. I think it was his demeanor. He was so quiet; so cool; so calm and so together. The money didn't hurt either, but back then I was much too young to really understand the role *that* played in a man's packaging. He chatted me up and was flashing his gold fronts and all. I hadn't really had much conversation with him.

I had always thought he was attractive and I'd heard about him but I hadn't had any personal interactions with him. I noticed him before Messy came into the picture, but we never got a chance to hook up. He would always just kind of look my way and give a hint of a smile, but that was all I got and all I ever gave in return. You know how anticipation can amp everything up and take it to another level? He was always so composed and tonight was no different. He was trying to get me to go home with him and honestly, it was working. All systems are GO! He told me that he had been hanging out with David in the club, but that they'd both driven separate cars. I'm thinking: This is great because he could take me home and my girl could do whatever it was that she and David were gonna do and there wouldn't be any issues with who was driving or being picked up in the morning or whatever. Bet! This was gonna be a good ass night. Yesssssuhh!

We all decided to go for a candle lit breakfast at Denny's. We returned to our posts on the hood of the car. Lip gloss was important and it started to fade from the milkshake I was killing. I went to the trunk of the car to grab my purse. When I got to the back of the car I stood on the parking block and leaned over into the trunk once I opened it. I wanted to be sure not to lock the keys in the trunk so I held them in my hand as I leaned in. When I stood up straight I dropped the keys on the ground.

Damn, am I still tipsy? I bent down to pick the keys up and I noticed that the asphalt from the new parking lot ran up against a small dirt floored tow yard. The dirt from the tow yard was peeking out from under a flimsy wooden fence that was doing a poor job of separating the tow yard from the restaurant. Little slivers of light shown through the cracks in the fence. I heard some crackling and hurriedly grabbed the keys and stood up. Probably a cat or something. I went back to the front of the car and we laughed and talked for a bit. About 30 minutes passed and the guys came back over to see if we were ready to go.

"Yeah, let's go." I was ready!

"Lil mama you wanna ride with me?" David is giving my ace some kind of silent signal that says, 'please come ride with me so I can have a few minutes alone with you before we eat'. She looks at me. I understand completely and I'm cool with it.

"Ok." She walks off all happy and shit.

"You can just follow me and I'll follow D." He turns to me and gives me that cool smile. He could've said sit on the hood of my car and hold on tight and I probably would have agreed.

"Ok. Hey, you want your purse?" Girl please, she was long gone. I got in my car and started it up. I saw her and David get into his car. He was parked across the street. My new boo was walking across the street too, but he must have parked farther down the street because he passed David's car and disappeared into the shadows. I knew his car so I waited to see him pull out into the street. First I saw David's car pull out and then … my boo. Before I could catch up, they both ran the red light and sped out onto the street to the left. I was too afraid to run the light so I sat there patiently waiting for it to turn green. I knew their cars and I knew where the Denny's was so I wasn't worried about it. My music was jamming and I was feeling right.

I reached over to turn up the music and just before my hand got to the knob, BAM! BAM! BAM! Oh shit! Somebody was banging on my window and pulling at my door handle. What the fuck? I look up and I see the last face in the world I wanted or expected to see. Messy Marvin. Oh My God! He is screaming and banging on the window so damn hard I thought for sure he would punch right through it. He was pulling the door handle and I could hear it clank against the car every time he let it go. What the hell was going on? Fuck! Where the hell did he come from?

"Open the muthafuckin door! Open the muthafuckin door right God damn now! You think you about to go fuck another nigga? That's what you think? I will kill you ass out here! Open the fucking door!"

"NO!" I screamed back at him from inside the car. I was not about to open that door. I knew I would be dead or beat to a pulp if I did. I was inside the car and I knew that was the safest place for me and I was NOT getting out. No matter what. I looked up at the light and it was still red. Shit! Fuck! I looked down the street to the left and I could see both cars speeding farther and farther away from me. BAM! He hit the window again. I heard

99

something other than his bare hand hit the window. I was scared for my life, but I had to think. No one was around. Checker's was closed and this fool would surely kill me if I didn't think quick.

"Open the fucking door or Imma smash this fucking window in. You hoe! You think you can fuck other niggas? I will fucking kill you bitch!" He was hitting the window with all his might. With every word he hit the window harder. Now I could have just run the light, I know, I know, but I was afraid to break the law. I was really thinking that. I was thinking that I could not go unless the light turned green. I knew what he wanted was a shot at me. He wanted to get to me. So I would give him what he wanted.

"OK! I will open the door if you stop hitting the window!" And then he stopped and there it was. The face of that sad, fucked up little boy. He stopped hitting the window and he took a step back. He believed me. He trusted me and I knew he'd believe me. He would probably be more fucked up than ever because I was about to betray his trust. I motioned for him to step back more. He hesitated, but then took a half step back.

His voice dropped, "You gonna open the door?" He was completely irrational. He knew it made no sense for me to open the door after that attack, but he wanted to believe me. He wanted to trust me. "You really gonna open the door? Huh?"

I hit the unlock button and made a motion like I was gonna open the door. Something must have clicked because he suddenly charged the car. He grabbed the door handle and I heard the door release from the jam. I felt a breeze of night air hit my arm. I hit the gas and the car jerked forward. I immediately hit the brake and the car rocked. I slammed the door shut and hit the lock. CLICK! When I looked up he was running toward the car again. He ran toward the front of the car before I could drive off. He slammed his hands on the hood and was screaming, but I couldn't understand what he was saying anymore. I put the car in reverse and punched the gas. The front tires must have been turned at an angle because when I hit the gas the car flew into the parking lot directly across the street from the Checkers. That parking lot was being refinished and there was yellow tape up around the entrance of the lot.

My car snapped the yellow tape. I looked up and I didn't see Marvin. That frightened me even more. I looked in the rearview window. The side view mirrors, but he had disappeared. Where the fuck did he go so quick? I wasn't going to hang around and see. Music was still blasting from my speakers and I put the car in drive and pulled up to the light. Fuck this, I'm running the light. I looked to the right and then to the left to see if I saw any cops. I eased the car forward so that I could see further down the street on both my right and left and I checked again for cops.

I looked back up to check the light and I saw headlights coming directly at me from across the street. It was Marvin's car! He was driving straight at me. Now, how the hell he got across the street and into his car that fast is still a mystery to me.

I FINALLY got some balls and ran that damn red light. I hooked a left and flew toward the Denny's. I was on one of the busiest streets in the city and even though it was the wee hours of the morning there was still traffic on the street. Even still, I was hauling ass! I was hoping that I could catch up with David's car. He was long gone though so I was going to go straight to the Denny's.

I knew Marvin was a coward and he'd never show his face around other men. I had turned the music down. I needed my mind clear. I saw Marvin getting closer and closer to my car in the rear view mirror. Damn this bastard is like a roach. He doesn't go away. I was scared, but because I had been away from him for a while his grasp on my mind wasn't there anymore. I was going to get away from him THIS night and he would not hurt me anymore. I drove like a bat out of hell and so did he.

If I made the light, he made the light and lucky for me, I was making them all that night. My adrenaline was pumping and I could feel the blood pulsating through my veins. I had to keep going. I heard his horn. He was blowing his horn and swerving behind me trying to get on the side of my car, but when he swerved, I swerved so he could never get his car beside mine. I wanted to keep him behind me. *I* was going to control this situation tonight. I came to a screeching halt. Caught at the light. Damn! Damn! Damn!

It was a major intersection and it was well lit. He did not care. He pulled up beside my car on the passenger's side and blew his horn like a mad man. He had all the windows in his box Chevy down and he was screaming at me. At one point he opened his driver's side door and put one foot on the ground as he threw his car into park. The car swayed back and forth and up and down on the shocks. Before he could get all the way out of his car, the light changed and I hit the gas. Hauling ass again. He cut the cars off that were behind me and he gave chase again. Damn this motherfucker! We sped through traffic. I stayed in one lane while he zig zagged in and out between cars trying to get in front of me. Before the next light caught us he pulled up on the driver's side of my car! I had been sure to stay in the inside lane so that he couldn't get beside me and force me off the road. He was actually driving on the wrong side of the road. He had the window on the passenger's side of his car down and he was yelling at me as he drove. He was weaving all over the street as the oncoming cars blew and swerved frantically around him.

I wasn't going to stop or be forced off my path, however, I realized that he was not going to stop either. He was out of his mind. I had my bearings about me enough to know where I was in town. I knew there was a police station near where we were. I decided that would be my best bet because I didn't know that I'd make it to Denny's with him driving the way he was. The police station was about 3 blocks up and to my left.

I came to the first through street that led to the police station and I whipped a left. His tires screeched behind me as he followed suit. It was dark on these little side streets and I knew my little compact car could accelerate faster than his heavy Chevy. At the next street I cut another corner and made a quick right. I could hear his engine behind me, but I didn't see his lights anymore. I thought I was losing him. Good! Finally!

I headed up the street in the direction of the police station. This damn neighborhood was like a maze. The streets were short and so dark. I made the next right and hit the gas. Out of nowhere I see headlights heading straight at me. I hear the familiar sound of his engine and I know I'm fucked. He must have gone down one of the streets next to me and come up to meet me head on. I was driving fast as hell and I hit the brakes and skid to a stop. He kept coming, picking up more and more speed along the way. I put the car in reverse and hit the gas, but he was coming way too fast for that to work. Shit! I hit the brake and turned the wheel. I had to turn my car around. I got halfway through my turn and it happened.

The chase had all been a blur. It had all been happening so fast. This … happened in slow motion. My car was sitting in the middle of the street perpendicular to his and he was plowing forward at full speed. His headlights were blinding me. Those have to be his brights. Then it happened. I closed my eyes and took my foot off the brake. I squeezed the steering wheel as he rammed into my car at full speed. The impact knocked me into the driver's side door. I could feel the car spinning and I opened my eyes to see my surroundings swirling around me. I saw the flash of Marvin's headlights as my car spun around. I opened my mouth to scream but I don't think any sound came out. Like in my nightmares. Suddenly the car came to a stop.

I quickly looked around and I was still in the middle of the street but now my driver's side door was in the path of Marvin's car. He put his car in reverse and his tires squealed. My head was throbbing and still spinning even though the car had come to a rest. I shook my head. Bad move. That made it worse. I heard the engine roaring again. I looked up and he was coming right at me again. This time he was going to hit me square on the driver's side door and T-Bone me. I had to try to move. I reached down to grab the gear shift. I was a fumbling mess. I looked out the window. He was still coming faster, faster, faster...I looked down again to see where the gear shift had disappeared to and I felt the impact...the crash was loud in my ear. My car slid across the road. The crash knocked my body toward the passenger side of the front seat. The seat belt chocked me and I gagged. I hadn't notice, but the seatbelt had slid over my shoulder during the first impact. I felt the gear shift under my hip.

This crazy son of a bitch is going to kill me. I have to get away from him. The headlights were still shinning into my car and I hear him screaming. He voice is loud as hell. Fuck he's out of his car walking toward me. I see the lights of the houses nearby come on. I have to get out of here. If he pulls me out of this car I'm dead. I know I'm going to die if he gets to me. I shift my weight back into the driver's seat and put the car into drive. I hit the gas hard but the car didn't move. The wheel weld was bent into the tire and the car was stuck. I turned the steering wheel hard in the other direction and hit the gas again. The car took off. I didn't even know what direction I was facing anymore. I just drove.

I came to the end of the street and I saw the street sign. I knew exactly where I was. The police station was just around the corner. I could make it. I could make it. I knew I could make it to safety. I was so close. I made the turn and I could see the station ahead of me. I slammed on the gas. I passed one intersecting street and then another as I got closer to the police station.

I was very aware that Marvin could catch me again. My heart thumped a little harder each time I zoomed past one of those side streets. The street I was on came to an end and I made the left that led me into the parking lot of the small police sub-station.

I pulled in and stopped the car. The night was jet black, but the lights at the entrance of the station were big and very bright. They were yellowish and fuzzy when they reached where I was sitting in the parking lot. Mixed with the darkness of night, it made my surroundings look gray. Like a gloomy, rainy day. I sat in the car and looked at the door to my safety. I turned the music all the way down and I just sat there in silence. I was breathing hard, my heart was beating a mile a minute and I noticed that my hands were shaking. I was shivering all over. I wanted to get closer to the entrance so I slowly pulled the car up to the parking spaces closest to the door. It looked like a picture book version of a police station.

The doors were black with panes of frosted glass in the center and they sat atop 5 or 6 large cement steps. There were two large wrought iron lanterns mounted on either side of the doorway. Above the doors the letters P-O-L-I-C-E were engraved into the stone overhang. I turned the car off. I gripped the door handle. The door creaked open. I was shaking like a leaf. I wasn't sure I'd be able to stand. I placed my left foot outside the car and let the ball of my foot touch the ground. I jumped and snatched my foot back inside the car and slammed the door shut. All in one quick moment.

My heart was up in my throat. I could feel every breath I took in my chest. His headlights slowly panned the parking lot and I was paralyzed with fear. I started to cry. I felt completely defeated. I could NOT get away from this monster! He was torturing me minute by minute and it was too much. I have a competitive side and I am a fighter, but hell, everybody gets tired and I was exhausted from it all. I was having a meltdown in the parking lot of the police precinct while my abuser drove by. All I could do was crouch down in the car and hope he didn't see me. It was too late, he had spotted me and he drove right by my car. All of me wanted to get out and run, but I knew that I couldn't make it to the door and inside before he could get to me and kill me.

The door to the precinct was locked and I knew that. My cousin used to work there and I had gone there before. I knew you had to be buzzed in. I would surely be dead before I could make it inside to safety. Taking into consideration the attitude of the last protector and server, I wasn't too confident in the local police. He rolled down his window and began screaming taunts at me. I'm sure he could tell that I was a crying blubbering mess in the car. I could hear him loud and clear.

"Get out the car bitch! Run and see if I can catch you! What you gon' do? Run inside the police station? Huh? What the fuck you gon' do now? You so fucking smart and slick and shit. Go 'head! Get out the car and see how fast I can run! Think I *won't* catch yo ass bitch! I'll kill you right here in the muthafuckin parking lot. I don't give a **FUCK!**"

As bad as it sounded, he was right. There was no way I could get to that door and inside to safety before he would be able to get to me and do whatever it was he was planning to do to me. I didn't know what to do. I was so ill equipped to deal with any of the things that were happening to me that night and during that entire time in my life. This fool was having a real 'King Kong ain't got shit on me' moment in the parking lot of the police station after he had tried to kill me with his car. WTF?

Chapter 8

'Ok girl, pull yourself together or you are going to die tonight. Fuck that shit! I will not die tonight. If I have to fight this savage off with my bare hands, so be it. My life has too much meaning for it to end like this. I am stronger than you and I have been beat down by you enough!' This is what I was saying to myself as he screamed at me like the fucking raving lunatic he was.

I think any woman that fights back, no matter how long it takes her to do so, has to get mad first. I mean pissed off, kiss my ass, go straight to Hell Ike - mad. I got that mad sitting in that car. I think I was so pissed because he thought he had defeated me. I felt broken and weak. As bad as it sounds I knew I could not make it out of that car that night. I decided to run. I had to get somewhere public. He wouldn't be seen acting out in public and he wouldn't be seen around other men behaving in such a way. I had to get myself into a public place or around some other men.

My new boo would be perfect right about now, but I'm sure they were ordering waffles and orange juice by this time. Something had to give. Shit! Where are the damn light bulb moments when you need them? For some reason he wasn't coming closer to my car. I don't know why he didn't walk up to the car, break the window and pull me out onto the ground and kill me right there. I really don't. He had plenty opportunity. He had plenty of time to do it and he could easily have killed me before anyone would've been able to get to me to save me. He had to be aware of that.

Abusers are cowards on lots of levels and I don't know if his cowardice got the best of him because we were at the precinct or what, but I know that I'm still here today because it wasn't meant for me to die that night. I had to get someone's attention. If someone would come out I could escape before he could get to me. He would definitely stall if he saw another person. That hesitation would give me the time I needed to get away from my car and inside. But, nobody was coming out.

HONK!!!   HONK!!!   HONK!!!   HONK!!! HONK!!!   HONK!!!   I blew the horn over and over and over and over again.   Either he would get spooked and leave, or someone would come out of the station.   Either way, I ended up safe. It was working. Yes! This son of a bitch was hesitating! Ha ha ha! Got yo ass, bastard! He had stopped yelling. He just stood there. He didn't know what to do.   HONK!!!   HONK!!!   HONK!!! HONK!!! HONK!!!   I was watching him, but I kept my hand on the horn.   All of a sudden he jumped in his car and threw it into gear.   I saw the doors to the station open.   Thank. You. God! Someone heard me.

The officer stuck his head out of the door.   I honked again. HONK!!!   Just to be sure.   When I saw Marvin's car leave the lot I jumped out of my car and ran up the steps where the officer stood.

"I need to come in! I need to come in!"

"Come in. Come in." He replied. "What the hell is going on out here? Who is that in the other car? Come inside."

"I need help. I need help to get away from him."

"Well let's go get you some help." He said it and he meant it and he shuffled me inside. After I went inside I told him the entire story and he sat and listened and filled out a police report. He didn't judge me. He didn't look down on me. He just did his job. When we finished inside he walked me outside and looked at my car so he could complete the traffic accident portion of the report. When all the formalities were done he told me that I needed to get a restraining order.

I didn't even know what a restraining order was. I asked him to explain it and he did. Basically, he told me that it was an Order by a judge that instructed Messy to stay away from me. I was a young, naïve girl who was not familiar with the ways of the world, but I knew damn well a piece of paper on file at the courthouse would not prevent this man from killing me the next time. I knew for sure that he would kill me. I had to protect myself in some other way because I was not ready to die. I took copies of the report and that was it. I was still left to face the night alone. He offered to drive me home, but I didn't want to leave my car there. And I was still ashamed in so many ways. I didn't want to have a police car drive up to my house for all my neighbors to see.

It hit me then. I can't go home! I'm sure he knows where I live. Where can I go? I didn't want to run back to my mom's house again either. He'd surely go there looking for me and she needed to know as little as possible about this latest incident. I knew he had fled and I knew he was afraid of the police so he most likely would not be back near that side of town tonight. I had to double think this bastard.

Nights can be long and this was definitely going to be a long one. I needed sleep. Real rest. My everything was exhausted. I got in the car and started it. The officer stood next to the driver's side of the car as I got in and he closed the door for me. He watched me pull off. In my rear view mirror I saw him walk back up the stairs and open the door to the precinct.

I drove onto the main road and prayed that I made all the lights. I didn't want to have to be sitting in traffic and risk him pulling up beside me. I needed to try to call my girl. I would have to tell her the truth about what had been going on and about tonight in particular. I wasn't too far from the hotel so I decided to go there. I knew it would be pretty quiet. No one around but the midnight auditor and I could use the phone and there was security so I would be safe.

I drove to the hotel in silence. I think I was still processing what had happened. The hotel had a driveway of sorts. There was an overhang that covered a circular drive thru right at the front door. The lights out there were bright most nights. Had the hotel been of any significant size, this driveway would have been where the valet picked up and returned your car. It was relatively small, but tonight it would have to serve as my fortress. Beside the outside border of the driveway was a wall of shrubs. The shrubs lined the small strip of gravel that separated the parking lot from the driveway. I pulled in right under the brightest part of the overhang, but I made sure to park near the decorative pottery outside so that the car wasn't fully visible from inside. Still hiding. I left my car running. I looked around before I got out. When the coast was what I considered clear, I got out, slammed the car door and ran inside.

The lobby doors were always unlocked. Thinking back that is unsafe as hell, but that's how it was. There was a security guard who was probably as useful as Barney Fife, but hey, he was a little bit of a deterrent, I guess. I rushed into the lobby and went to the doorway that led into the back office. It was locked. I rang the bell. The sleepy faced night auditor appeared from the back office. As night auditors go, they are generally weird. I've yet to meet a normal one. And Rick was no different. He looked like he was a cat in his former life. Thin; malnutritioned; bad comb over; crazy funky breath; and long nasty looking yellowish nails.

"Hey."

"Hey Rick. I just need to use the phone real quick."

"Yeah, no problem." He handed me the phone over the counter. Who knows what the hell he had going on back there so I didn't question why he didn't let me back. I just graciously took the phone and dialed. It rang and rang and rang. I figured she wouldn't pick up. Damn. I hit the receiver and dialed again. Same thing. Ring after ring after ring after unanswered ring.

"Everything alright?" Some people are so damned nosy and Rick was in the 'some' crew. He worked overnight and was always questioning what was going on during everyone else's shift. So I'm sure this pop up by me in the middle of the night (in my club attire) was like catnip to his creepy, nosy ass.

"Yeah, I'm good. Just lost my friends during the drive. Trying to catch up with them."

"Oh. I just don't usually see you here at these hours. Ya know?" Yeah bitch! I know! Stay out mine and get your own business. Damn!

"Yeah, I was close. Do you know where the nearest Denny's is? Is there another one besides the one by the car wash?"

"Well there's that one by the water, but that's way outta your way, I'm sure." He stops and looks his nosy ass at me for some kind of insight. Straight poker face. Dude answer the damn question and get you some business. For real. This is sad.

"Is that the only other one?" I ain't falling for that BS.

"Those are the only 2 I know about."

"Ok. Thanks Rick. Have a good night." I handed him the phone and started to walk out.

"You need me to walk you to your car?" He was coming from behind the desk.

"Nah, I'm good. I parked under the lights right here. Thanks though." I can barely shake him. Let me hurry the hell up and get outta here before I have another chase on my damn hands. I hurried through the lobby and out the door. I got to the car and pulled off just as Mr. Need-Me-Some-Damn-Business got to the lobby doors. I saw him waiving behind me, but I was not hardly gonna stop. Where to now? I drove around the back side of the hotel just to get out of Rick's sight. I hadn't really worked out a Plan B. And I think I had a damn good excuse for not having planned ahead.

"Shit!" I was cursing at myself in the car. I didn't have any idea what I should do. "Shit! Shit! Shit!" I had to go back inside. I needed to use the phone again. I made a wide U-turn in the parking lot at the back of the building. I decided to park on the side of the lobby out of Rick's sight so I could disappear more quickly this time if I needed to. Who am I kidding? *WHEN* I needed to.

I parked in a spot on the side of the lobby near the shrubbery and decorative pottery. It wasn't even really a parking spot. It was more like a small slab of concrete between the building and the start of the legitimate parking lot. I pulled all the way up to the building. From the front of the building you couldn't even see my car. This is all for you Rick. All for your nosy ass. I turned the car off and looked around again. There was a car that pulled up under the overhang. A man turned off his lights and jumped out and went inside. I waited. I knew he wanted a room, but I also knew Rick was a lazy bastard and would come up with some way to deter the man so he wouldn't have to do any real work. There was a Motel down the road. He'd be fine.

Sure enough about a minute later, the man walked back out and poked his head in the passenger's side window. While he was talking I saw the headlights from another car approach on the opposite side of the driveway. Man, why is it so busy tonight? And why the hell is it so busy right at this moment when I'm trying to escape an abusive, murderous lunatic? It was creepy as hell sitting in that non-parking spot in the dead of night waiting for a free moment to run inside and use the phone. The guy was still talking and the second car had pulled up even closer to the front of the man's car. I couldn't see anything but headlights from the second car. Whoever it was, they were being extremely rude. If I can see their lights from here I'm sure the people in the car under the overhang had to be blinded by the headlights. Apparently the man wasn't bothered because he went back inside when he finished talking to the passenger. The second car backed up and then swirled through the parking lot. I wanted to see what kind of car it was. Who was being so rude?

I lifted myself off my seat to get a better view. You ain't even gonna believe this shit. It was Marvin! Damn, he came to my job looking for me? What would have led him here? I ducked down in my seat and watched his headlights round the front parking lot. He didn't circle the entire building or he had already done so before I had looped back around and parked. I think I almost pissed my pants when I saw him. I have to get out of here and go somewhere he doesn't know about. I waited a few more minutes and looked up to see which direction he'd headed. Good, he was going to the post office. Dumb ass! I took off in the opposite direction.

116

This game of cat and mouse was for the fucking birds. I had to go ahead and shut it down. I was trying to talk myself up. It wasn't working. Besides going in the opposite direction I had no clue how to ensure that I'd be safe throughout the night. As I drove I decided I needed to go somewhere he either was unfamiliar with or didn't know about.

I didn't want to do it, but I headed to my girlfriend's house. Marvin didn't know where she lived or who else lived with her. He was a coward so even if he found her house I knew he'd never approach the door because there could be a man inside and he wouldn't face a man. I drove to her house and pulled into the driveway. I couldn't knock on her mom's door because I wasn't sure if she had made it home yet. So if I show up at the door without her, her family would be worried. Damn! I just sat in the car. I know what you're thinking, but this was before cell phones. Or at least before cell phones were like they are today. I had one, but I used to leave it on my dresser at home all the time. It was a different time.

Her house sat in on an open lot so I wasn't too afraid of being attacked there. I was afraid that she may not come home for 10 more damn hours, though. I did feel some kind of calm sitting there. I could get inside the house if I needed to and I knew that at some point she would come home. So I just sat there and waited. The porch light was on and I knew my surroundings pretty well. It wasn't that bad. I would end up sitting there all night. I saw the sun start to peek over the clouds and I couldn't have been happier. You know the freaks come out at night and daylight means they take their asses back into the holes they crawl out of at night. I started the car and inched forward a few feet. SCRAPE! SCRAPE! SCRAPE! I stopped and got out. I wanted to see how bad the car looked. It looked like a giant had played patty cake with it. It was crumpled on both sides. Poor car. *sigh*

I drove slowly so that it would be full on daylight by the time I got to my mom's house. And it was. I parked my car in the grass because my brother's car was in the driveway. Great! I went in and immediately hit the bed. I knew I'd be awakened soon enough. I didn't dare go to my own place because if this guy had been watching me, which I suspected he had, he definitely knew where I lived. A couple hours later I hear commotion outside. I got up and threw on some sweats; ready to deal with the aftermath and my family. My brother bolted through the door and stormed down the hallway. He proceeded to beat the bathroom door to death. I was brushing my teeth and I ignored him. He beat and I brushed. When I finished I opened the door and before he could get anything out, "Let me get dressed so you can take me to the police station. Give me 10 minutes." His eyes were frantically scrolling up and down my body. He thought I was hurt. And had I looked at my car I would have assumed the person driving was hurt as well. I got dressed and grabbed the police report and restraining order information the officer had given me. I walked into the living room where my mom and brother were conferencing.

"Let's go. I'm ready."

"You got everything you need?"

"Yeah." We walked to the his car and got in. "I need to get a disposable camera on the way back so I can take pictures of the damage." He shot me an alarmed look and scanned me up and down again. "The damage to the car. I'm alright." He looked back at the road.

"What are you gonna do?"

"I want out. I want this to be over for good and I want him to leave me the hell alone. I want my life back. This shit is crazy the way it is now."

"Yeah." He took a long drag from the cigarette he had lit at the last stop light. He held it for what seemed like an eternity. I think I was holding my breath waiting for him to exhale. He rolled down the window and blew the smoke outside as we drove at a steady pace toward the police station. We didn't speak any more. We pulled into the same precinct I had been to the night before. It was the closest one to my mom's house. Inside the receptionist told us that we were in the wrong place. We had to go to the State Attorney's office and take the report I had from last night and any other information or evidence and request an injunction against him.

"So what happens after that? How long does that take? What can she do in the meantime?" He was rapid firing questions at her. She wasn't moved by it at all.

"Sir here is the address and this is the floor you need to go to when you get there. They can answer all those questions for you at this location. Anything else?" He snatched the paper and started toward the door. I looked at her through the bullet proof glass and mouthed 'thank you' she nodded and gave a half smile. When I got to the car it was already running. He was pissed. It was Saturday which meant we had to wait until Monday before we could even file the paperwork requesting the injunction. This guy was manipulating and controlling not only my life, but now my family's life and time as well. He had a hold on my entire existence. And we hadn't even been together that long. We didn't have kids. We weren't married. Our money wasn't comingled. All those factors played in my favor and it was still a complete nightmare trying to get rid of this asshole. The sooner you make a move, the better. That was what I thought. I would learn later that the safer you make a move, the better. We drove back home feeling defeated and unimportant in the eyes of the system.

"What's wrong?" My mom asked as soon as she felt the vibe we dragged in the door with us.

"She gotta wait til Monday when the State Attorney's office is open. So we gotta sit it out over the weekend."

"So what do we do until then? She's just supposed to be hold up in the house like a hostage til then? The laws on this ain't worth the paper they're written on!"

"Yeah, I know. You can't go back to that apartment. You just gotta stay here." I hadn't planned on it, but I had done some pretty irrational things so I could understand why he felt he needed to say that to me.

"Yeah. I'm trapped here. I know." Even though I appreciated their concern, this shit was happening to me. Nobody else in that house had been choked out, punched, cursed out and humiliated by this bastard. It was me. So although the biggest secret of all was out, I felt more alone than I had before. All eyes were on me now and I was the one who had to face all this and overcome it. Their support would help a lot, but I had to do it by myself. I got up and went into the bedroom.

The day progressed into the evening and after dinner I settled in for a comfy wumfy session of T.V. and snacks on the couch. I had my favorite quilt my grandmother had made for me when I was a baby, I had the remote control and I had a full belly. Perfection. My brother came into the living room to ask me if I needed anything. I told him no and he left to run to the nearby store. While he was gone my mom came into the living room.

"Wake up. He's outside." I woke up disoriented a bit. I don't know how long I'd been sleeping.

"Huh? What? Who?" That must have been some good sleep because who the hell else would she be talking about?

"Marvin! He's outside acting a fool!" She was pissed more than anything else.

"Where is he? What did he do? How long has he been out there?" I had snapped back to my miserable reality and was in full Messy Marvin mode.

"He out there flashing his lights and blowing the horn like the fool he is!" While she was talking I heard his horn. He was really going fucking buck ass wild! He has lost whatever little bit of his mind he has left. He was at my *mother's* house acting like this.

After all that had happened? Who does that? Oh My God! He had pulled his car up to the edge of my mom's driveway so that his headlights would shine into the bay window of my old bedroom. He was flashing his bright lights off and on, off and on, off and on. He was laying in on his horn and honking like a maniac. Lights and horn at the same damn time! Who does that? Huh? I wanted to turn into a man for 20 minutes and just go out there and beat his motherfucking ass! You can't come to my mama's house and cut up like this. I knew he had to have been watching the house too, because he waited until my brother was gone from the house to do this. Coward ass punk. Does he really think I would come outside after last night? Does he really thing I wouldn't call the cops?

"How long has he been doing that?" My mom was pacing at this point. Her nightgown was blinking from his headlights. The widest part of his headlights were lighting up the edge of the living room where she stood. This shit is way too much. You got my mom out of her bed pacing back and forth in her own house. Nah, dude. This is gonna end.

"Let's just call the police." I felt so guilty, like I'd caused all this. I kept thinking that I should have left sooner or that I should have told them sooner or not ever have been with him. How could all this come to be just because of some stupid, skinny ass, fucked up dude? Suddenly it stopped. The noise of the horn and the flashing lights. I heard the car pull off fast. Then I heard my brother's car damn near come through the living room. He was in the house in 2.2 seconds.

"Imma go get that punk ass nigga! I can't believe he came here after all this shit! He came here? He came here? This nigga is really crazy! Then he runs when I pull up. Just like the punk that he is!" I couldn't even look at them anymore. I was so wracked with guilt. This shit was all fucked up and it was all my fault. Now he was torturing my family. What if the neighbors heard all that? Damn, they would know too. It was just embarrassing and I felt so low. I went back to the couch and pulled the quilt over my head. I wanted the night to be over, but I didn't want to face tomorrow – at the same damn time.

Chapter 9

The next morning while we were eating breakfast in silence, this fool pulls his car into my mother's driveway and actually gets out and knocks on the front door. If I hadn't lived this, I wouldn't believe it myself. The mental and emotional portion of an abusive relationship is often times as bad as being popped in the eye. I felt so much guilt and shame already and then the fact that he would not stop and was now involving my mom and brother and damn near the whole neighborhood, was just guilt on top of guilt on top of embarrassment. This was all my fault. That's what you think and that's how you feel. You feel like a fuck-up. I started to doubt my own judgment. I doubted my own intelligence. And my own worth. How could I have been so stupid? How could I not have known things would get *this* out of hand? Why didn't I see any signs? Was this happening to me because I deserved it? What had I done in my lifetime to deserve being in this situation? Why is he outside right now?

My brother threw his fork down and went to the door. He slammed the door behind him as he walked outside. "Aye man! What the fuck is yo problem bruh? You must be crazy coming here after what you did to my sister last night. What you want, man? What you want?"

Then punk ass, "Hey man I don't want no trouble. I just wanna talk to her. I heard she was in a car accident last night. I just came by here to make sure she was ok and everything." If I had a camera right now I would look dead in the lens and ask you if you hear this shit. Unfucking-believable, right? I know. I lived it. You know how a person can be so mad that they get really, really calm? Yeah, that's where my brother was. My mom and I looked at each other. It got quiet for just a few seconds longer than we were comfortable with. I heard my brother say in a calm voice "Man get in your car and get the fuck out my mom's yard before I fuck you up and end up in jail for killing yo lil' ass in this driveway. A'ight man? Do that, bruh." He stood there until asshole got in his car. He was smirking and talking, but he was walking his cowardly ass back to his car. My brother came back into the house and sat at the table in front of his plate. "That nigga crazy. He's fucked up. He got some real problems." He was talking to his plate. I just tried to finish eating.

"Did I hear him say he was coming to see how she was doing?" My mom was questioning.

"Yeah." He seemed annoyed, but she kept going.

"Like he didn't know what happened, huh? He asked about a car accident too, didn't he?" She wasn't letting up.

"That's what he said." He murmured under his breath.

"Hmph! Ain't that nothing?" My mom was definitely from the South.

"We going first thing in the morning, alright?" He was looking at me now.

"Ok." I couldn't even think of anything else to say. I was completely embarrassed and ashamed of myself. How could I be so stupid?

Monday morning we were up bright and early and headed to the State Attorney's office. My brother had become my full time chauffer and body guard, it seemed. He took me everywhere. My car was drivable still, but I didn't like being in it. It reminded me of him and it looked horrible. There are cars in traffic every day that have dents and dings, but I felt like people were looking at me and that they knew why MY car was banged up the way it was. I can't reiterate enough how deep the psychology of abuse is. The effects of someone physically controlling you with violence and fear affect every part of your life: from the most tiny, seemingly insignificant thing to the most prevalent part of your existence. There is just no escaping it. We made it there and went inside. There was a small smug reception area that was lined with plastic chairs and dusty pictures and certificates on the walls. The clerk sat behind a long bullet proof window. There were diagonal stripes that crisscrossed all over the glass. On the lower part of the glass was a small circular cut out just big enough for her voice to seep through. "Can I help you?" Her voice was as flat as the glass.

"I need a restraining order." She turned and ruffled through some papers. She turned back to the glass and slid something under the glass to me.

"Fill this out and come bring it back up to me when you finish. There are pens and clipboards over there." She pointed. I took the papers and filled them out. As I read I learned that what I was doing was actually asking the court if they *would* issue what is officially called an Injunction for Protective Order. The process was this: I would complete a set of documents including a description of the things that had happened that caused me to fear for my personal safety; those documents would make their way through the court system until they reached a judge; the judge would decide whether my situation warranted a court order instructing Messy Marvin to stay away from me; if it did; then the Sheriff would issue Messy a notice of his court date and we'd appear in court where we would both have an opportunity to explain; the judge would make a decision; if the judge decided - yes, Messy would be served with a court order outlining the details of the Order of Protection; if the judge decided - no, my ass was even more SOL than I was before walking into that office. Lord Jesus take the wheel!

Here's to hoping I could convey fear onto a sheet of paper. I filled out the forms until I came to the pages where I had to outline why I needed protection from this fool. My first thought was that I wanted to *tell* someone these things instead of writing them down. But the more I thought about the things he'd done to me, the more appreciative I was that I didn't have to repeat them out loud. I wrote it all out. I talked about the first slap and the fight we had in my mom's living room; him breaking into my mother's house; the knife to my neck, being choked into unconsciousness; the slaps; being punched in the head; being drug across the living room and the carpet burns; the time he wrote down the serial numbers of the pack of condoms we used to make sure I wasn't cheating;

the humiliation of him making me stand in the bathroom while he choked me with one hand and put the fingers from his other hand inside my vagina because he thought he could "smell another nigga" on me; this idiot sitting outside my mother's house blowing his horn non-stop; the showing up at my mother's house the next day; and of course the car chase and crash. I wrote all of it down. It took a long ass time, but my thought was that I needed the judge to know exactly how crazy he was. I wanted to be sure they all knew what I knew, which was that HE WOULD KILL ME! He had tried and/or threatened it on more than one occasion.

Everyone's first question is always, "why didn't you leave?" What most folks don't know is that women are at the highest risk of injury or death when they leave an abusive relationship. Abusers are controllers and a woman leaving is the ultimate symbol of their loss of control. The abuse that occurs within the relationship is usually a result of feelings of minor losses of control or an expression of dominance by the abuser. When a woman leaves the relationship that expression of dominance and feeling of loss of control is multiplied exponentially.

These men are not stable minded creatures. They are emotional shit storms themselves. They do not have the tools necessary to respond appropriately to the loss of a woman they think they love or possess. So they react with an escalated level of violence that often times ends with them killing the woman who has tried to escape. It's not as easy to leave as people think. I wouldn't have understood it either if I had not lived through it.

When I finished filling out the forms I took them back up to the window. I gave them to the receptionist along with the copy of the police report. She took them from me and told me someone would call me within the next 48 hours. That's the other thing about getting out of an abusive relationship safely - the time delays constantly put you at risk. First, I had to wait until Monday morning. Now I would have to wait another 48 hours.

Many women don't have a safe haven during this time or money to live for a week or two while the system does its thing. This is a very dangerous time. Luckily for me I had a safe haven. I had a job, I had family members and I had a chance at getting out safely. It's difficult, but it IS possible. The 48 hours passed and I stayed my ass at home! I didn't go to work or to school, or anywhere else alone, for that matter. A couple days passed and I received a call from the State Attorney's office. They asked that I come back down to the office. I has a hearing date and they wanted to explain the process to me. I went back down to the State Attorney's office. I met with a woman who explained to me that Marvin would be able to defend the claims I had made against him.

I didn't understand that because I wasn't asking for him to be arrested, I only wanted to be protected. Apparently, because I was asking the court to prevent him from being near me he had a right to explain to the court why an injunction should not be entered against him. I was shocked. So he could ask and maybe have the court agree that I should NOT get a restraining order? What the fuck? What would I do then? Move out of the country? This was craziness to me. I couldn't digest it.

She went on to explain that due to the accusations I'd made the State Attorney had decided to pursue charges against Messy. The exact charges were not clear yet, but I would be kept apprised. From there I was ushered into another office where I met with a victim's advocate.

Her office was a mess. There were papers strewn all over the desk and piles of papers were stacked on the floor. The chairs even had papers and files piled in them. She cleared a spot for me and quickly explained the Victim's Advocacy program. The program would keep me updated with any charges, court dates or responses from Marvin that were related to my case. I was automatically enrolled in the program because the State Attorney had decided to pursue criminal charges against Marvin for the car chase and crash. Had I not had housing, food or employment, they would have helped me with those things. I left feeling completely overwhelmed. I had a court date. I had loads of information. And I would have to come back.

In about a week (more time, I know) I had to appear in court. I was scared to death. I didn't know what to expect. I didn't want to see him and I had no idea what he would say or what the judge would say. My brother on the other hand, was ret ta go! On the court date, we got to the courthouse and there were a gazillion people sitting outside the courtroom in the waiting area. My heart was beating so fast. I thought he'd walk in at any moment. Finally the bailiff comes out and starts to escort us into the courtroom. It was a giant cattle call. Everyone on the docket that day was seated in the courtroom and the judge called out the cases one by one.

I sat next to my brother in the pews. That's what it felt like. The seats were the same as church pews and just as hard and uncomfortable. I sat on the inside of the row we were on. Closest to the wall and my brother sat beside me. The room was wide and the judge's bench was quite a ways away from where we sat. I didn't know at the time, but Messy was outside waiting for our case to be called. He was a coward and I should have known he wouldn't face my brother after he knew I'd filed for a restraining order and that this was serious. Each time the court room was quieted for the next case to be called I had a mini panic attack.

Finally my name was called. Messy walked into the courtroom. My brother looked at me. "There he is. Punk." Oh Lord Jesus! My brother nudges me in the arm, "go ahead." I stand and excuse my way through the sea of knees. When I got to the end of the row I almost ran into Messy. I was a mess. He stepped ahead of me and stood to the right side of the podium that sat just below the judge's bench. I walked up and stood as far away from his as possible. The judge asked if either of his had representation and before I could answer, here goes this ass, "Yes, sir. I have a lawyer." A thin white man approaches from behind us and joins him on his side of the podium. They whisper to one another and the judge looks at me.

"Ma'am are you represented here today?" I was confused. Was I supposed to have retained an attorney? No one told me that in the State Attorney's office. Where the hell was my advocacy now? Was the judge going to deny my request because I didn't have an attorney? "Ma'am?"

"No sir I don't have an attorney." Marvin snickered under his breath. So mature, right? The judge looked at him over the top of his glasses. "Are you representing the defendant today counsel?"

"Yes your honor, I am."

"Ok, let's see what we have here." The judge started shuffling through papers and it looked like he was reading. "So ma'am you want an Order of Protection?" "Yes."

"Are you afraid for your safety?"

"Yes." I tried not to, but I hung my head and looked at my feet. I wanted to disappear. I felt like everyone was looking at me and now they all knew that I was afraid of him because he'd beat me. I felt their eyes on my back as I was forced to stand there and face this whole situation.

"And sir you would like me to deny her request for an Order of Protection against you? Is that correct?"

"Yes...." his 'attorney' interrupted him. "Your honor my client doesn't feel that an Order of Protection is necessary. He has no intentions of contacting the Plaintiff. This is simply a relationship that has ended that the Plaintiff can't handle. If anyone needs an Order of Protection it's my client. The Plaintiff has been harassing him, your honor."

What the Jesus, Mary and Joseph! I know this motherfucker did not just sit here and let this man say that I was a threat to him. I jerked my head up and my mouth was gaped wide open. Marvin whispered something in his ear again. "She is calling my client non-stop your honor and he is at risk of losing his job because of what's been going on."

"He's lying!" I blurted out. "I don't contact him at all. He's come to my mother's house twice and he ran into my car while I was sitting in it. He's lying!"

"Counsel do you have any proof that she is harassing him?" The judge seemed annoyed.

"No your honor. My client was just served 2 days ago and didn't have adequate time to…"

"I've heard enough." He *was* annoyed. "Are you requesting I issue a restraining order against her as well?" As well? Did he say as well? That must mean I'm going to get my restraining order. Thank God! I wanted to smile, but I knew that wasn't appropriate.

"If your honor is going to issue an Order of Protection against my client, then yes, we request the Court issue a reciprocal Order."

"If your client wants a reciprocal order he will need to go through the proper procedure and request an Order and have it set on the nearest docket. Today I will grant the Order of Protection to the Plaintiff and I will tell your client that he needs to tread lightly. I have read the documents enclosed here today. Both parties should not leave until you have seen the clerk on the way out and are both provided copies of the Order." He looked over at me. "Ma'am I suggest you familiarize yourself with the Order and follow up with Victim's Advocacy before you leave today." Damn, now they all knew for sure that he'd whipped my ass before. I nodded, "thank you." Messy was still standing there with his lawyer. I walked toward the pews again as my brother stood up.

Messy was behind me and it was an eerie feeling to have him behind me knowing he wanted me dead or really fucked up and knowing he would do it if all these people were not in here. My brother met me at the aisle and asked if I was ok. I shook my head yes and kept walking. I just wanted all those eyes off me. It was too much. I was so embarrassed. That was the last time I'd see Messy face-to-face. At the time I didn't know that. If I had, I probably would have been more at ease.

I went toward the clerk's office, but a lady came and escorted us to a different room away from him so there wouldn't be any contact. I was given the Order and some accompanying documents that explained what to do if he violated the Order. Basically it was a completely useless piece of paper and the reality of that was not lost on me. I knew that if he wanted to get me he could and in the time it would take me to get to a phone, I would be dead. He knew it too. As I walked away from the clerk's office my eyes met his.

He looked right through me. His nostrils flared and he threw his head back and squinted his eyes at me. Then he just laughed and looked down at the restraining Order and laughed again. I knew what message he was sending me and I was truly afraid. The thing is this: I was living in a perpetual prison of fear and trepidation. My brother couldn't be with me every minute of the day and it was obvious that he would lie in wait and pounce the first chance he got. I was afraid all the time, even when I was with my brother or in my mother's house. How would I know that he wouldn't snap and burst through the front door with a gun? What could we really do if he broke into my mother's house in the dead of night with a gun?

Nothing. That's the answer, nothing. He'd broken in before so I knew he could do it again if he wanted to. My only solace was the hope that his cowardly ways would keep him outside because he knew my brother was inside the house. That was no real peace of mind. I left the courtroom with my flimsy protection and went back to my mother's house.

Chapter 10

Things remained quiet over the next couple weeks. I went back to work, but I had to tell them about the situation so that they were all aware. I also worked days whenever possible instead of my regular 3 p.m. to 11 p.m. shift. The seasonal job at the post office was over and I'd decided to take a break from school for a while. I started to spend some nights at my own apartment with my brother, but I was still messed up and scared to death. I had met with the victim's advocate I'd been assigned and she was there if I needed help with things, but for the most part I felt very alone and on my own still. I can't imagine how women survive who don't have the support that I had. It makes sense that so many go back. It's hard. Especially when you're starting from zero.

A few more weeks went by and I got a call at work. It was the State Attorney. I went down to her office and sat in the waiting room for what seemed like an hour. Finally she came out and got me. We walked back to her office and I had a seat. She looked very professional and she sounded very stern when she spoke. She told me a lot during that meeting. I found out that the State had decided to press charges of aggravated battery and assault with a deadly weapon against Messy. The deadly weapon was the car. They had wanted to charge him with attempted murder, but felt the assault and battery charges were more likely to stick. I was totally fine with that. I was scared, but my spirit was still strong underneath it all. I was no weakling and I wanted him in jail so that I could fucking relax for a change. She explained that I might have to testify against him. That scared me.　　　　The thought of the courtroom with all those people was not something I was looking forward to doing again. But apparently this would be different. There would only be the jury. I still didn't want to have to face him and tell anyone what he did. Be it 12 people or the 75 that were waiting in that first cattle call. She told me I'd have to tell her everything. EVERYTHING. There were still things I hadn't told anyone. There were things I hadn't put in that documentation requesting the restraining Order. There were things I hadn't thought about since they happened because I wanted to bury the memories. She told me I had to resurrect them and bury them after he was prosecuted. So I started to spill. I talked and she wrote. She wrote and wrote and wrote. At times she interrupted and asked questions and then she wrote some more. I told it all. From the first blow to the final crash. At one point she stopped me and asked, "Do you realize you've been sexually assaulted as well?" Who? Me? Sexually assaulted?

"No I don't feel I've been sexually assaulted. I mean he was rough sometimes, but I don't feel like I was raped." She cocked her head to the side.

"Tell me again about him choking you during oral sex." Oh, that's what she meant. I started to rush through it, but she made me slow down.

"I was in the shower and he came in. This is when we lived together. He said he wanted me to suck his dick like a prostitute. I told him I didn't know how to do that and he said I would after he finished with me. When I got out of the shower he was in the bed. I got into the bed and he told me to get on top of him. I straddled him on the bed.

137

He had me lean forward so that I was face to face with him and my hands were flat on the bed holding my body weight up.

He took his fists and hit my knees and knocked me off balance. I fell on top of him and he slid my body down the length of his body. He grabbed my shoulders and pushed me down further so that my face was in his crotch. He told me to put his dick in my mouth. I did it and he told me to keep my teeth off it and move my head up and down.

Where do I put my tongue? I had never done it before and I didn't know what I was doing.

'Just do it! Damn! You always got a million fucking questions! Don't act like you ain't never sucked a dick before!' Before I could respond he had grabbed my chin and slid his dick in my mouth. I clamped down and he pressed his fingers into my jaw and my neck and tilted my chin up. 'No teeth!' I opened my mouth wider and he slid it in further. I gagged and he pressed into my jaw and my neck again. 'Don't gag until I tell you to.' I tried to shake my head, but he wouldn't loosen his grip. He slid his dick in my mouth again and I tried not to gag so I put my tongue up against the roof of my mouth so that he couldn't put it all the way in.

Well, apparently that was a bad move. He put his legs around my torso and slid me off the bed. 'Get on your knees on the floor.' My body was already off the bed so I just went with it. He spun himself around and stood above me. He grabbed my bottom jaw again and pulled down. I opened my mouth and he slid it in.

Forcefully this time. He jammed his dick in and out of my mouth while I gagged and chocked. I couldn't move because he was holding my head. I wanted to bite down on it and make him bleed, but he held my bottom jaw so that I couldn't clamp down. Tears were streaming from my eyes from the force of his thrusts and from me gagging. He pulled himself out of my mouth and turned to cum on the bed sheets.

I fell to the floor and tried to catch my breath. My whole mouth hurt. My tongue felt rough from the back and forth thrusting and the roof of my mouth was raw. 'You should be glad I didn't nut in your mouth like I wanted to.' I ran into the bathroom and sat on the toilet in the dark and cried. Eventually I went back to bed and we never spoke about it again. Later he would tell me that he didn't want head from me because I didn't know what I was doing and his dick had bite marks from me trying."

She shook her head and said, "That is sexual assault. If you didn't know that before, now you know." She said she'd go through all her notes and my prior police report and then notify me of the final set of charges. Since I was the victim in these crimes, I would have to sign off on the charges before they were filed. I left and waited for the call.

It came a few weeks later. I was ok with the charges and I went back to her office to sign off on them. While there I learned a lot about Marvin that I did not know. He had been charged with domestic violence against a former girlfriend in a nearby city a couple years prior. While in the city we lived in, he had also beaten up his son's mom. Yeah, his son! I didn't even know this negro had kids! Well, he did. He had not one, but 3 kids! ***Three!*** And get this, he was much older than he had always told me he was. He was like 10 years older than I was. So this was a grown ass man doing all this sick shit to me. He was really fucked up. He had also beaten up the girl he dated just before me. She had filed charges against him, but he'd gone to her house a few days before she was to testify and had damn near killed her. He had beaten her so badly that her jaw had been wired shut. She dropped the charges and would not tell doctors who had caused the injuries to her jaw.

He was clearly an abuser. A straight up woman beater. Oh yeah, and the night he chased me down with his car, he had been lying in the dirt of the tow yard that bordered the restaurant parking lot. He was there in the dirt listening to my conversation with the guy the whole time.

None of the women before me had put his ass behind bars. They probably felt all the things I was feeling. Shame, guilt, embarrassment and fear. I wasn't going to back down though. It wasn't because I was stronger than any of the other women. I was going to follow through because I wanted him in jail so I'd have time to develop a plan to get myself safe. Truly safe. I knew that if he was around he wasn't going to leave me alone long enough to really detach myself from him completely.

I couldn't have that monkey on my back like that. I had to shake loose. I told them I was willing to do what I had to do in order to help them prosecute him. From there things were out of my hands. The State Attorney took over and I was given updates through the victim's advocacy program.

Most of the updates were by mail and none said what I wanted to hear which was that they had issued a warrant and arrested him. I did get a phone call, however, informing me that Marvin had filed a lawsuit against me.

I almost don't want to write this. There is so much shit that happened it's almost too much to tell. But, yes, it's true that yet again Messy Marvin was messing with my life. He filed a civil lawsuit against me demanding that I pay him back for any money and other items he gave me while we were together. As if I owed him anything. Can he pay me back for all those damn licks I took? Well apparently I would have to show up to court and explain to the judge that the things he'd bought for me or given me during our relationship were gifts. At that time under the law of our state, gifts could not be recouped. I was done with dude. I was so over him with his vice grip around my life. Let him have his moment in front of the judge and let him try to recover while his ass was behind bars for assault with a deadly weapon.

I refused to entertain him. I didn't respond and he actually won the case against me by default. Yep! He was awarded an amount equal to all the money he was able to prove he had spent on me. Do you know this dude had kept all the receipts from every dollar he spent on me since we met? I didn't give a fat baby's dick either. Go straight to hell Ike! Whatever!

I finally got the call I was waiting for. There was a warrant issued and they arrested him. Finally. Now what? Now he would have an opportunity to respond to the charges against him. He denied them all and plead not guilty. The State offered him a plea deal and he turned it down which only prolonged the process. I learned that had the other woman followed through with the charges, he would have been facing a much harsher sentence for what he did to me. But, since they had not, it was like starting from scratch. It was as if this was his first offense. This meant he would likely get less time than, I felt, he deserved.

The back and forth with him and the State Attorney over the plea deal continued. Ultimately, he declined the deal and decided to take his chances with a jury. Of course, I wanted him to take the plea so I wouldn't have to appear in court and testify, but I figured he would be an asshole about the whole thing. Asshole behavior was the norm for him. What's new? I was meeting with the State Attorney periodically to prepare for the trial.

As the trial date approached she told me that he started to waiver and was now interested in talking about a plea again. This was just a couple weeks before the start of trial. By the time we were a week away he was practically begging for the plea deal. Soon I was told they reached a deal. He would get 4 years in jail. I still, to this day, don't know how I feel about that. He did a lot of shit to me and I definitely didn't want him to harm anyone else, but I just don't know. 4 years was enough time for me to form a plan to permanently escape and to execute it. I left the State Attorney's office knowing I would be able to finally breathe again.

In the time he was in jail I finished school, moved to a new apartment and got a new car. I put the drama of that relationship behind me and there came a time when I didn't think about him every single day. Eventually, the fear subsided and I stopped looking over my shoulder every other second. I went back to a normal life. Things were good. I went to work, ran errands, ate, slept, shit, you know all the normal things you do.

A few years passed. I was in the grocery store one day getting some groceries and I decided to get a Lotto ticket. I never played Lotto, but why not? It might be my lucky day. I was standing at the kiosk bubbling in numbers on the Lotto form with that little baby ass number 2 pencil they give you. I felt like I was taking a scantron test. I chose my numbers and went to get in line. I stopped dead in my tracks. There he was. Messy Marvin. In the flesh. He walked in through the automatic doors of the store and I was literally frozen. I could not move. I felt my bladder tingling. I almost pissed in my pants from fear. I was so afraid. My body was shivering.

I threw the Lotto form down and ran out of the grocery store. I ran to my car and pulled off as fast as I could. I hadn't thought about the fact that he would be released one day. I wanted to be out of the state by the time he was released. Why didn't I know he was out? I called my mom who told me that I did have some mail at her house. I had used her address because I didn't want my address in the court file for him to access. I went straight to her house and sure enough there was paperwork that had been mailed to me stating the date of his early release. I knew I had to get the fuck outta

Dodge. I was just as afraid in the grocery store as I had been when I was trapped in that apartment with him.

Even today when I see someone who resembles him I feel the flush of fear flow from my head to my toes. I did move and now live in a place where I feel safe. It's been over 10 years since this all happened to me, but in that time I have known women who haven't been as lucky as I was. Some have died and others are still living in misery.

Domestic violence is very real. It happens to the strongest of women. It's very much misunderstood. Even today. I want women to know that they can learn some of the early warning signs and if they do find themselves in an abusive relationship, there is help and safety out there. When you save a woman you save a generation. There are women who need to know they are worthy of being saved, and that there are people who care enough to help save them. There is life after.

As for Messy Marvin, he's still out there somewhere. I heard he dated a girl after me who he beat down in the middle of the street with an aluminum baseball bat. He had told her not to come outside, but apparently the phone rang inside the house and the call was for him so she stepped outside to let him know about the call. Word is, he flipped out and beat her right there in the street in front of everyone. I don't know if that's true. It's just what I heard, but I wouldn't be surprised if it were true.

I don't know why I fought back and I don't really know why I survived. I just know that I did and I'm no different than the next woman. No woman should endure what I endured and every abused woman deserves a chance at life.